MisLeading Lady

Sharon Y. Judie

Written By Sharon Y. Judie

Published by: Pen Legacy®
Cover Design by: Junnita Jackson

ISBN 978-0-9600483-0-4

Library of Congress Cataloging – in- Publication Data has been applied for.

Acknowledgments

I am thankful to God for His abundant mercy and grace; to my amazingly supportive husband, Carl, for loving and encouraging me when I embarked upon this venture; to my children, grandchildren, parents and siblings for having my back and making me believe that I can do anything; to my publisher, Pen Legacy and Charron Monaye for inspiring me to get this book finished. Thank you to my BFF, my Gurlz and everyone who has cheered for me along the way. Your words of inspiration fueled my desire to see this through to completion.

Much love and may God's best blessings rain upon you always.

PREFACE

Writing this novel has been an amazing journey. MisLeading Lady is based on my original stage play of the same title, which debuted in 2017.

The response to the story of Pastor James Miller and his wife, Lady Vivica Miller, has been phenomenal and I'm very excited that this book is the first of a series of stories that I pray you will add to your list of must-read books.

Prologue

She sat on the edge of the toilet; her head and right shoulder were propped against the bathroom wall. Her thoughts and worries seemed to disappear each time she filled her lungs with smoke from the glass crack pipe that she always kept hidden in her bathroom cabinet. She'd been sitting in that same position for the past hour, until she heard the sound of frantic knocks on the bathroom door.

"Mommy! I have to use the bathroom! I can't hold it anymore!" Her six year old son cried.

"What?" she yelled loudly.

"Mommy, I really have to go!" He whimpered again.

She stood up and walked out of the bathroom, and Devin rushed in past her. Once Devin came out of the bathroom, she rushed to get him and her three year old daughter, Mya, dressed and out of the door for school. They would be late to school once again.

Several hours passed quickly, and she had spent most of the day getting high. When she looked at the clock on the stove, she realized it was almost time for her children to return home from school. She took two more hits from her crack pipe and then she sat down on the couch to wait for her children to get home. A few minutes later, her doorbell rang. She opened her door to greet her children, and she was startled to see Mr. Harvey, the principal of Jordan Heights Elementary School, standing behind Devin and Mya. Mr. Harvey looked into her eyes and he sensed she was high on something. She immediately looked away from him. "Y'all go inside now," she told her children.

They obeyed and quickly walked past her and into the apartment. Her eyes quickly darted back to Mr. Harvey. "Yes?" she said, looking directly into Mr. Harvey's eyes. She had her arms folded across her chest.

"Ms. Davis, I'm not sure what's going on and I'm trying not to pry, but…"

"Well, don't pry." She interrupted him mid-sentence. "Just mind your business." She was angry that he was being so nosey.

"It became my business a few days ago when I noticed Mya had been coming to school in dirty clothing. She keeps asking for seconds and thirds at breakfast time, as if she's not getting dinner at night."

She stood silently, looking downward to avoid his questioning stare. She was gathering her thoughts and thinking how she wanted to respond to him. She then slowly looked up. "Mr. Harvey, thank you for being concerned, but don't be." Then she closed the door before he could respond.

Later that night, as she was sitting in her bedroom getting high again, she was consumed with guilt about being a better addict than she was a mother. In that moment, she made the decision to leave. She packed a few belongings and walked into the living room holding her duffel bag. She stood in the doorway in silence, staring at her children as they watched TV. Her kids eventually noticed her standing there watching them. Devin was intuitive and sensed something wasn't right.

"Mom, where are you going?" he finally asked.

"Honey, Mommy is leaving. She needs to get herself together. I need you to be a big boy and take care of yourself and your little sister," she responded, while tears streamed from her eyes.

"Mommy, Mommy, please don't go!" Devin and Mya were both crying. She stood there as tears continued rolling down her face and onto her blouse. She had already made up her mind; she left and closed the door behind her and locked it.

Devin and Mya were confused and they were scared. Devin hugged his sister and they cried themselves to sleep. The next morning when he woke up, Devin hoped that the previous night's events were a dream. He got out of bed, tiptoed to his mom's bedroom and quietly pushed her door open. She wasn't there. It wasn't a dream. She had left them.

At six years old, Devin was extremely smart, so he did what he had seen his mother do many times before. He woke up, got dressed and then he woke up Mya and helped her get dressed. Mya sat at the table and watched quietly as Devin took two bowls and two spoons from the sink and rinsed them with dishwashing liquid and hot water. He removed the carton of milk from the refrigerator and set it on the table. He dragged his chair across the floor and used it to stand on so that he could reach the box of cereal in the cabinet. He poured the cereal and milk into the bowls and he and Simone ate in silence before leaving for school.

When they returned home after school that day, Devin opened the door to the apartment, hoping their mother had returned. That wasn't the case. For the next two days, Devin and Mya conducted themselves as if their mom was there with them. They went to school. Came home. Ate dinner. Went to bed and started over again. On the third day after their mom left, Devin and Mya returned home from school and were frightened to realize that the electricity had been turned off. Devin consoled Mya and hugged her tightly when the sun slowly gave way to the dark night. To make matters worse, they had eaten the last bit of cereal that morning and the refrigerator was empty. Every few minutes Mya quietly cried and said she was hungry. Devin was hungry, too, but he didn't know what to do. They both went to sleep with severe hunger pangs.

Early the next morning, Devin went to the small market at the corner and stole a package of lunch meat and tucked it under his coat. He ran home and woke up Mya, shared the lunch meat with her. Because the electricity was shut off, Devin wasn't sure what day it was nor what time it was. They missed the next two days of school.

Although their mother was a drug addict, she ensured her children attended school every day, so on the third consecutive day that Mya and Devin missed school, Mr. Harvey went to check on them to make sure everything was okay.

He walked up the dimly lit hallway that led to their apartment and he took a deep breath, as he anticipated their mother's annoyed reaction to his presence again. Instead, when he knocked, Devin slowly opened the door and Mr.

Harvey immediately noticed the tears in his eyes. Mya stood nervously behind him. The mini blinds were closed and the apartment was dark, but the large fluorescent security light outside the apartment window provided enough illumination for Mr. Harvey to see that the children's faces looked dirty and that Devin was wearing the same shirt and pants that he had seen him in when he attended school the previous week. Puzzled that the children had opened the door and not their mother, he called out to her. "Ms. Davis. It's Mr. Harvey. Can I come in? Ms. Davis, can I come in?" Devin instinctively stepped aside to let him in. Mr. Harvey stepped inside and continued calling out again. After quickly scanning the dark apartment, he realized the children were home alone and it was apparent that they had been for several days. Mr. Harvey immediately took out his cellphone and dialed 9-1-1.

The bright sun warmed her face as she exited the Second Chance Rehabilitation Center. The heavy door shut loudly behind her. The shabby, run-down white building had peeling paint and needed a fresh coat of paint. This had been her home for the past 30 days. 30 days without drugs. 30 days without her children. She didn't have a desire for the taste of the crack cocaine that had controlled her life for the past five years. Her heart beat fast as her thoughts turned to scooping up her children in her arms, planting wet kisses on their faces and begging for them to forgive her for leaving them.

Her thoughts were interrupted when she saw the local city bus approaching. She reached inside her purse to find her wallet and counted enough change to pay the fare for the bright blue bus that would take her to within walking distance of her apartment. After she paid the bus fare, she sat down in the vacant seat behind the driver; her thoughts raced as she wondered if her children were ok and if they would forgive her for leaving.

The bus ride seemed longer than it normally did, so when she reached her destination, she exited the bus and began quickly walking, then running, toward her apartment. She put her key in the lock and unlocked it. She opened the door and called out to her children. "Mya! Devin! Where are you? Mommy's home." Her children were not in the apartment, and it was apparent they hadn't been there for a while.

Chapter One

The sun had just set when Darrelle pulled into the parking structure where his fiancé, Keenya, lived. They had been engaged for almost a year and he loved romancing her. He was going to surprise her with a dinner cruise around the marina. It was mid-summer and the weather was perfect. The weather was always nice in Los Angeles. He parked, set his alarm and then walked the two flights to her apartment.

As soon as she opened the door, he sensed something was wrong.

He kissed her gently on her cheek and gave her a hug.

"Do you want to talk about it?" He asked.

She hesitated for a few seconds and then finally spoke. "I called and asked my father for some money to help pay the money I owe to the IRS and he acted like I had asked him for a kidney. You know I wouldn't have called him unless I had no other choice. I'm so over him."

"At least you can call your old man when you want, even if all you do is argue with him. I don't even know who my dad is," Darrelle said.

"I'm sorry, babe. I wasn't thinking. I apologize for being insensitive," she responded.

"Don't worry about it," he told her.

"If I didn't have my mom, I don't know what I'd do," Keenya added.

"Your mom is the real deal," Darrelle said.

"She loves you like you're her own son. The first time she met you, she told me you were going to be the one that I would marry."

"Really?"

"She sure did. It's almost like she has a sixth sense. She has a heart of gold and sees the best in everybody. She really is my best friend."

"I envy the relationship you two have," Darrelle confided.

"My dad wasn't there for me, so my mom picked up the slack for him and never complained. There's no love like a mother's love," Keenya reflected.

"So I hear," Darrelle responded quietly.

"I'm sorry, Darrelle. You know how close I am to my mother. I can't imagine what it was like growing up without yours."

"It's all good, baby," he assured her.

"You've shared so little about your past and I know it bothers you to talk about it. But if we're going to spend the rest of our lives together, I really need to know who you are. I'm not trying to pry and I'm not trying to push. You can trust me enough to share those dark details of your life. Who are you, Darrelle Brown?" She pried.

"Who am I? That's a good question. Where do I start?"

"Start wherever you'd like and start whenever you're

ready. I've got you." She cupped his hand in hers and quietly waited for him to open up and share his feelings.

Darrelle inhaled deeply. "I think I'm ready. I hope you're ready."

He closed his eyes, whispered a prayer and then began to share.

Chapter Two

The Governing Board of Love of God Christian Fellowship was engaged in small talk, waiting for Pastor Miller to arrive.

The traffic on the 405 Freeway had slowed to a crawl and Pastor Miller was a little distressed that he was late to the special board meeting that he had requested. Traffic was barely moving and he was hopeful that the Board members wouldn't be too upset with him for being tardy.

The Board was an outspoken group of six eclectic individuals. First, there's the outspoken Deacon Henry Edwards. A short, round, bald man, with a scruffy gray beard and gray sideburns. He is no-nonsense and quick to remind everyone of *church protocol*. Next, is Robyn Fremont, a quick-tempered woman in her early 40's. She is a newer church member, who is not far removed from her street-savvy ways. She is quick to argue and always ready to fight. She wears her jet-black hair parted down the middle and she never changes her look, always sporting two long French-braids on either side of her head. Her nemesis and the object of most of her arguments is Pastor Miller's mother, Helen Miller, affectionately called *Mother Miller*. Mother Miller is in her early 70's, but her beautifully smooth, wrinkle-free, walnut complexion makes it difficult to guess her age. She is quick-witted and not afraid to speak her mind.

Marva Campbell, affectionately called "Miss Marva", is the church mother and prayer warrior. She exudes kindness and extends grace to everyone. Her graying temples hint that she's a senior citizen, but she still has a lot of spunk and a kind word for everyone.

Jaden Miller is the youngest of the bunch, and being that she is the daughter of Pastor and Vivica Miller, some of the other members overly-criticize everything about her. If she wears a dress, someone complains that her dress is too short. If she wears pants, someone complains that her pants are too tight. She often feels stifled by church politics, but she does her best to make her parents proud and by all accounts, she is a good girl.

Rounding out the board is Mrs. Vivica Miller. She is the essence of class and beauty. She wears the title of *First Lady* well. Her caramel-hued skin glows and it is always flawless. She is strikingly beautiful, even without much make-up. Always elegant and impeccably dressed, she is well-spoken and she looks like she was born into wealth.

She and Pastor Miller met on a blind date that was arranged by a mutual friend almost 30 years ago. After many phone calls back and forth, their first date was at a popular breakfast spot and they have been inseparable since that first date. She was attracted to his smile and charisma. He was down-to-earth and loved doting on her. He was attracted to her zeal for life and her quiet demeanor. They were perfect for one another.

He was attending the local university when they met and she had recently been honorably discharged from the U.S. Air Force, after serving four years. They dated for almost two years before he asked her to marry him.

Pastor Miller's father had performed their wedding ceremony before 150 family and friends. Their wedding was intimate, but very romantic. They were affectionate with one another and still very much in love. Their daughter, Jaden, had moved into her own apartment, so they were enjoying their new freedom as *empty nesters*, until Pastor Miller's mother moved in approximately a year ago.

Pastor Miller parked, got out of his car and hurried inside. "Good evening everybody. Please forgive me for being late. Let's open with prayer and go ahead and get started," he spoke quickly.

"It's ok, Pastor," everyone chimed, as they bowed their heads and closed their eyes to join him in in prayer.

"Father, we seek your presence as we discuss finances and other issues that are affecting this church. Give us clear direction and instruction as we seek Your will. In Jesus' name. Amen."

"Amen." Everyone responded as they raised their heads and gave Pastor Miller their attention.

"Thank you all for coming to this special call meeting this evening. What I have to talk about won't take long." He began, while taking some papers from the folder he was carrying. He passed around the agenda to everyone. He cleared his throat before continuing. "Our first order of business is to discuss the financial state of the church."

Deacon Edwards raised his finger to interrupt and then stood up, looking directly at the Pastor. He straightened his tie and his glasses, waiting to be acknowledged.

"Yes, Deacon Edwards. Do you have a question?" Pastor Miller asked.

"Let me say this, Pastor. I know this is only your third board meeting as our new pastor, but I would like to remind you that when Rev. Hatfield was the pastor, he always discussed finances last, not first. So, as the young people say, *'I'm just sayin'.'"* He then took his seat and folded his arms and they came to rest on top of his round belly.

"Thank you for your input, Deacon Edwards. If you give me a moment to explain, you'll understand why I want to discuss our finances first." Pastor Miller told him. Pastor Miller was holding an envelope in his hand. He opened it and pulled out a letter and unfolded it. He looked around the table at everyone and then glanced down at the letter he was holding.

"I received this letter from the bank yesterday, stating that there is a lien on the church and that our church will be put up for sale soon," he spoke solemnly.

Everyone began looking at one other in disbelief and talked quietly among themselves.

"So, let me guess. You're going to bail on us like Rev. Hatfield did," Robyn finally spoke.

"No, Sister Robyn, I'm not. When the members here elected me as pastor, I felt that God had answered my prayer. I know that this church has great potential and I believe that God is going to use me to take this church to the next level."

"I heard that Rev. Hatfield said the same thing when he got elected as the pastor. It sounds like he took this church to a new level– right to the bottom." Robyn spoke out again to

Pastor Miller.

"Robyn, please hush and let him speak. Good grief!" Mother Miller snapped at Robyn before she could finish her tirade.

Robyn just stared at Mother Miller, without responding. Mother Miller, unintimidated by Robyn's cold stare, locked eyes with her without blinking. Pastor Miller took the opportunity to continue talking while the two ladies were silent.

"As I was saying, I would like for us to come up with some ideas to raise funds to bring our note current."

"Raise funds? We wouldn't have to raise funds if everyone gave their tithes. I count the offering, so I see what everybody gives every week," Deacon Edwards said and shook his head disappointedly.

"Deacon Edwards, you know we can't force people to give," Pastor Miller told him.

"It is my recommendation to require all members to sign a contract committing to give their tithes," he replied.

Sis. Vivica coughed before speaking. "Deacon Edwards, with all due respect, I hope you're not serious."

"Yes, I'm very serious. Everybody needs to pull their weight." Deacon Edwards told her.

Sis. Robyn looked at Deacon Edwards before addressing him, "Deacon Edwards".

Deacon Edwards looked at Sis Robyn, "Yes?" He responded, eager to hear her voice her agreement with his suggestion.

"Every time you open your mouth, you remind me of what my grandmother used to say, "it's better to be quiet and be thought a fool, than to open your mouth and remove all doubt. Good luck with that contract," she told him.

"Come on, everybody. Let Pastor finish going over the agenda," Miss Marva insisted.

Pastor looked approvingly at Miss Marva. "Thank you, Miss Marva. What I was saying is that I would like to discuss some ideas for fundraising."

Before anyone else could speak, Jaden rushed in and quickly took a seat. "Sorry that I'm late, Daddy. I got stuck in traffic."

"That's ok, Jaden. You haven't missed too much," her dad assured her.

"No, you only missed the part about your father wanting us to start selling hot dogs or something to raise money," Robyn exaggerated.

"You know that's not what my son said, you crazy woman!" Mother Miller Mother quickly replied.

Robyn stood to her feet, staring at Mother Miller, while taking off her earrings, indicating she was ready to fight. After placing her earrings in her chair, she began swinging her arms like a windmill. "You know what, Mother Miller? I've had just about enough of you and that mouth of yours. I don't mind fighting old people and little kids. Y'all are easy wins!" Robyn shouted.

Mother Miller started swinging wildly at Robyn.

"Mom! Robyn!" Pastor Miller yelled, to get their attention.

Robyn immediately stopped and quietly sat down, but Mother Miller was amped up and continued swinging, trying to hit Robyn.

"Come on, Robyn. Get up and take this beating. Please don't let this gray hair fool you. I'll beat you like you stole something!" Mother Miller threatened.

"Ladies!" Vivica shouted.

"Mom!" Pastor Miller repeated loudly.

Mother Miller finally stopped swinging and sat down. She was breathing heavily and sweating.

"I'm sorry, Pastor, but she started it and I don't have a problem finishing it. I know that she's your mother, but she starts a lot of trouble. She knows she's too old to act this foolish," Robyn said.

"Son. Deacon. Sis Vivica. Sis Campbell. Jaden." Mother Miller looked at each of them and apologized. "I'm sorry. I don't know what got into me."

"The devil got into you, as usual," Deacon Edwards replied.

She quickly shot a disapproving look at Deacon Edwards and enunciated each word for emphasis as she spoke, "Don't start today, Deacon." She raised her cane and pointed it toward the Deacon. "You picked the right one, but the wrong day. I'm warning you." It was apparent that Deacon Edwards enjoyed pushing her buttons and upsetting her.

"Lady, if you don't have a seat and knock it off. You probably don't even know what day it is. Talking about *'right one, wrong day'*." Deacon Edwards chuckled.

"Don't let my sweet smile fool you, Deacon Edwards," Mother Miller told him. "I can go toe-to-toe with the best of them. I'm not a pushover."

"Daddy! What on earth is going on in here with all this arguing?" Jaden asked.

"Tensions are kind of high today, baby girl. I just announced to the board that the church may be put up for sale soon."

"Why? What happened?" She asked.

"Apparently the mortgage wasn't being paid long before we got here and the church is in foreclosure. We need to focus on raising funds pretty quickly," Pastor Miller said.

"Pastor, we usually have good success with bake sales," Miss Marva added.

"Pastor, we need to *just say no* to bake sales. The last time we had a bake sale, somebody made some "special brownies" (he added finger quotes for emphasis), and let's just say that everyone with glaucoma and cataracts got healed that day," Deacon Edwards eagerly responded.

"Oh, my!" Sis. Vivica exclaimed.

"I don't know how I missed the brownies," Miss Marva said innocently.

"Miss Marva! Really?" Sis Vivica said as she tried to suppress a cough.

"Wait, no, I didn't mean it like that! What I meant was I didn't hear about the brownie incident," Miss Marva replied.

"Well, that's a first, because nothing usually gets by you, Miss Marva," Robyn asserted.

"You're getting a little too sassy, Sis. Robyn. Watch yourself," said Miss Marva.

Pastor glanced at his watch. "It's getting late. Let's discuss some ideas and see what we come up with."

"Daddy, remember at our previous church when the youth hosted that *Electric Slide Marathon* to raise money to pay for the registration fee for kids who wanted to attend the state youth conference?" Jaden asked.

"I sure do. Several churches participated and it was a lot of fun." He responded.

"If you dance with the devil, eventually he's going to

want to lead." Deacon Edwards said.

"Deacon Edwards, we would never do anything questionable. Everybody joined in the fun. Even the Mother's Board auxiliary danced. We had a blast!" Vivica added.

"Come on, Granny. Let's show him," Jaden said to her grandmother, as she assisted her to her feet. Mother Miller stood up slowly and the two began to do the *Electric Slide*. After she "dipped" twice, Mother Miller experienced pain in her hip and quickly sat down, as Jaden continued dancing. Mother Miller managed to smile while rubbing her aching hip.

Deacon Edwards sat quietly, looking at Mother Miller with disdain, while shaking his head back and forth. He then looked a Pastor Miller, wondering why the Pastor wasn't offended by what they had both just witnessed. "Dancing has no place in the church," Deacon Edwards finally offered.

"I hate to admit this, but I agree with Deacon Edwards. I'm really not for all that dancing and carrying on in the church. Why don't we think about hosting a gospel concert or something like that?" Robyn offered and broke the silence.

"That's a great suggestion, Sis. Robyn," Pastor Miller agreed.

"I love gospel music! I have a friend who is a Christian rapper." Jaden offered.

"I'm not going to even share my thoughts on what I feel about that suggestion," Deacon Edwards countered. "I really can't believe that we are even entertaining the thoughts of singing and dancing in the church, to raise money. I guess your next suggestion will be that we put up a dancer's pole!

And one more thing. All that jumping around and yelling that some of these so-called singers do is a shame and a disgrace!" Deacon Edwards exclaimed.

Jaden looked at Deacon Edwards, astonished by his response. "Well, since you don't like that idea, can we make it a spoken word concert? We could invite some other churches to participate," Jaden offered.

"That's a good idea, too, Jaden. This may be the perfect way to appeal to the youth in this community." Pastor said.

"I think we can do it, if we all work together," Vivica interjected, while suppressing a cough.

"I'll agree with anything right now. I'm ready to go. We've been here all night! "Robyn exclaimed dramatically.

Mother Miller looked at Robyn and smacked her lips and shook her head.

"Mother Miller, I was not talking to you," Robyn said.

"I didn't say anything," Mother Miller quickly responded to Robyn.

"That's the best decision you've made today," Robyn said, while exchanging glares with Mother Miller.

Pastor Miller's request to Jaden broke the tension between the two women. "Jaden, why don't you draft a tentative outline for the concert? Deacon Edwards and I will look it over and we'll take it from there," Pastor Miller offered.

"Will do, Daddy. I'll work on it and get it to you by tomorrow afternoon," Jaden told him.

"Perfect," her dad smiled. He looked around at everybody. "That wasn't too hard, was it? Now, are all minds clear? Vivica? Mother? Sis. Robyn? Sis Marva?"

Pastor Miller asked. Everyone responded by shaking their heads to indicate they had nothing more to offer.

"Ok, if there's nothing else, let's stand, join hands and dismiss with a closing prayer. Deacon Edwards, do you mind leading us in prayer?" Pastor Miller asked.

Deacon Edwards hesitated a moment before responding. "Pastor, I want to make sure that you and this Board know that I'm not real happy about this fundraising idea. I would really like my tithing contract idea to be considered."

"Deacon Edwards, please meet me here in the morning around 9 or so, and we'll discuss your concerns." Pastor replied.

"I hope you're not going to try and change my mind and get me to accept this foolishness, but I'll meet with you, Pastor. Thank you for offering to take the time to meet with me. I am much obliged. Now, if everyone will bow their head and close their eyes, I'll pray," Deacon Edwards spoke in a low tone.

Dear Father of Abraham, Isaac and Jacob. Our Wheel in the Middle of the Wheel. The Great I Am. Our Lily of the Valley, and Bright and Morning star. Our Rose of Sharon. It's me, It's me, it's me, oh Lord, standing in the need of prayer. It's not my mother, and it's not my father. But, it's me oh, Lord, standing in the need of prayer. We thank you for every blessing you have ever bestowed upon us. Hear your servant's prayer. In the name of the Father, and of the Son and of the Holy Ghost, thank you, God! Amen! Goodnight, everybody" he said, while placing his hat on his head.

"Good night." Everyone responded in unison.

Robyn yelled out for everyone to hear, "A dismissal prayer should be short and sweet, Deacon Edwards! Please keep that in mind in the future!"

Deacon Edwards didn't respond to her, but Robyn was content because she had told him what was on her mind, and possibly what everyone was thinking, but didn't dare say.

She got in her car and sped towards her home. Deacon Edwards waved to everyone as they left the parking lot. When the last car exited, he locked the gate and got back in his car. His old sedan sputtered as he slowly got on the expressway and drove toward his home.

Chapter Three

Vivica hadn't been able to sleep, and for the past three or four hours, she had been forcing herself to keep her eyes closed. She finally got out of bed, put on her robe and went downstairs to the kitchen to start a pot of coffee. As the coffee was brewing, she walked over to the stereo system and put in the gospel CD that she had recently purchased. It was 6:45 A.M. She had planned on sleeping in, at least until 8 or so. She began quietly singing to the music. When the coffee was finished brewing, she poured a cup and sat down on the couch. She had so much on her mind. She drifted in thought as she sipped her coffee and quietly meditated and prayed. She enjoyed the quiet stillness of the early morning.

Meanwhile, upstairs, Pastor Miller reached over to cuddle a few minutes with his wife, but he was disappointed to find that she had already gotten up. He knelt on the floor beside the bed and prayed before showering and getting dressed. He could hear the sound of gospel music quietly playing as he started walking downstairs to greet his wife.

"Good morning," he said when he saw Vivica sitting on

the couch, enjoying her coffee.

"Good morning." She smiled.

"Why are you up so early?" He kissed her on the cheek.

"I couldn't sleep because of this cough." She responded, while coughing. "I'm going to make an appointment with Dr. Douglas as soon as I can.

"Good. I'm glad you're finally going to get yourself checked out. You've had that cough for a while." He looked down at his watch. "Anyway, I need to get out of here. I am supposed to meet with Deacon Edwards in about twenty minutes. Wish me well."

"You know I always do. Call me and let me know the outcome of your meeting with him. And, don't forget that I'm taking your mother to the doctor today." She added.

"I know you told me, and I apologize for forgetting, but please remind me of what this appointment is for again?" He asked.

"It's just her regular annual check-up."

"Good. I appreciate you chauffeuring her around. I know she's a handful, but try to have fun."

"Pray for me," she joked.

"You know I will" He told her, while hugging her tightly. "I'd better go. Deacon Edwards will have a fit if I'm one minute late," he said before picking up his keys and heading to the door.

"Alright, see you tonight." Vivica was quietly meditating when her mother-in-law entered the living room. She was fully dressed; she had her purse in her left hand and her right hand on her hip. It was apparent she was ready to leave.

Vivica looked at her and smiled faintly. "Granny, why

are you dressed so early? Your appointment is not for another three hours."

"It's better to be early than late." She frowned. "I'm not like you, Vivica, showing up late all the time."

Vivica didn't respond, but she gritted her teeth and shook her head at her mother-in-law. The elder Mrs. Miller had moved in with them while she was undergoing chemotherapy for breast cancer one year earlier. Although she and Vivica seemed not to like one another, they secretly admired one another's strength. During Mother Miller's recent bout with breast cancer, she noticed how resilient she was. The chemotherapy caused her to lose her hair and it made her weak and sick, but the elder Mrs. Miller never complained.

Mrs. Miller studied Vivica, from head to toe, before speaking. "I know you're not wearing *that*, are you?"

"No, ma'am. You do realize these are my pajamas, right? I got up and made some coffee and I've just been sitting here relaxing. We have plenty of time. Do you want me to make some breakfast before we go?" she asked her.

"No, thank you! I'm trying to stay well!"

"Granny, I know you didn't mean that," she chuckled.

"I'm sorry, sweetie. You know my *dementious* flares up unexpectedly and I'm liable to say anything. You know that."

"Yes, ma'am I do know you're liable to say anything." Vivica whispered under her breath.

"Excuse me?" Mrs. Miller responded harshly, staring hard at Vivica.

"I said, *'I'm going upstairs to get dressed.'*"

"I don't think that's what you mumbled, but, yes, go and

get dressed," her Mother-in-law replied.

"How about we stop somewhere and have breakfast before I take you to the doctor?" Vivica asked.

"You know I don't have much of an appetite these days. Besides, eating all that greasy restaurant food upsets my stomach. I don't mind sitting with you while you eat, but I'll just have a cup of coffee or some tea," she responded.

"The diner on the corner has a senior's menu that you might like," Vivica teased.

"The diner on the corner? I'm not a *diner on the corner kind of woman*, Vivica, and you should know that by now. If you insist on taking me to eat, I'd rather have something filling." She reflected for a moment before continuing. "I really could go for some Cajun-style shrimp and grits!" She exclaimed.

"Shrimp and grits?" Vivica questioned, while frowning.

"Is that a problem?" Mother Miller asked, as she peered over the top of her glasses.

"No problem at all," Vivica relented.

"Go and get dressed, sweetie. We don't have all day," Mother Miller scolded.

"I'll be right back." Vivica went upstairs to get dressed and returned a short time later. She was always stylish, even when she wore casual attire, and this day was no exception. She looked comfortable, yet classy in a sleeveless, red floral maxi dress, that she paired with gold sandals.

As they were leaving the house, Vivica set the house alarm, and, as was their normal practice, Mother Miller walked down to the end of the long, winding driveway to wait for Vivica to back the car out of the garage and pick her up. This short walk from the house to the driveway was getting more challenging because of tendinitis in her right knee, but despite the pain, Mother Miller was determined to remain as active as she could.

Although she cherished her independence after the death of her husband a few years earlier, the elder Mrs. Miller knew in heart, that moving in with her son and daughter-in-law was a wise decision, while she underwent treatment for cancer. Her bedroom, which was spacious, and impeccably decorated, was adjacent to the family room and overlooked her cherished rose garden. Her son, James and his wife, Vivica, never made her feel like she was a burden. Their home was truly her home, too.

The Millers lived modestly and didn't spend money frivolously, so Vivica was pleasantly surprised when Pastor Miller presented her with a pearl white Mercedes CLS550 to commemorate their 30th wedding anniversary a few months earlier. She loved driving it and, for the most part, she really didn't mind chauffeuring her mother-in-law wherever she needed to go. Mother Miller was a mother figure to her. She had lost her own mother when she was a child.

After driving a short distance, the elder Mrs. Miller's face lit up when Vivica turned into the parking lot of a popular soul food restaurant that they frequented. A short time later they both enjoyed a nice, hot bowl of spicy shrimp and grits.

When they were finished eating, Vivica paid the bill and drove Mother Miller to her appointment. Mother Miller received a clean bill of health and to celebrate the good news, they left the doctor and went to lunch. Mother Miller had talked Vivica into taking her to the new chicken and waffles restaurant that had recently opened.

Vivica was still full from the breakfast they had eaten less than two hours before, so she didn't order anything to eat.

She watched in amazement as her mother-in-law ate three wings and a huge waffle. She silently whispered a prayer of thanksgiving for her mother-in-law's appetite being restored. She had recently been praying that God would help her see the good in every situation. Yes, she and her mother-in-law disagreed on most issues, but she was glad that God had spared her life.

When they finally made it home, the elder Mrs. Miller said she was tired and she retreated to her room to take a nap.

Vivica went upstairs and lay across her bed. She was exhausted, too.

Chapter Four

Deacon Edwards arrived at the church an hour before his scheduled meeting with Pastor Miller. After parking his car, he walked around the church grounds and picked up pieces of trash. He turned on the sprinkler system to water the lawn in front of the church. He then pulled out some of the weeds that he noticed in the flowerbed.

He was sweeping leaves from the courtyard when Pastor Miller arrived. Pastor Miller waved at him after he got of his car and walked toward the church. He had just started brewing a pot of coffee when Deacon Edwards walked in his office.

"Thanks for meeting with me today, Pastor." Deacon Edwards said and reached out to shake hands.

"No problem, Deacon Edwards. If something concerns you or any of my members, I have an obligation to make sure we are all on the same page. Before we get started, I want you to know that I appreciate your commitment to this church," Pastor Miller stated.

"My commitment is first to God and then to the church.

That's why I can't understand all this crazy stuff that you are trying to bring in here!" Deacon Edward told him.

"Deacon Edwards, please understand that I will never allow anything disrespectful to happen here. I believe that the direction our church is headed is the direction that God is pleased with. I'm asking you to trust me, ok?" Pastor Miller requested.

"I put my trust in God always, never in man," said Deacon Edwards.

"Understood," Pastor Miller answered.

"Church people think they have to go along with everything so they can get along with everybody. We weren't meant to fit in. We were meant to stand out!" Deacon Edwards interjected.

"I agree with you, but let me add that we can't be afraid of stepping outside the box and praising God in a different way." Pastor Miller said.

"You call it stepping outside the box, but we are jumping right into the Devil's playground! Look, Pastor. I don't want to take up too much of your time, and I don't think we're going to reach a reasonable conclusion." Deacon Edwards told him. "I just want to make sure you know how I feel about these changes that you're implementing."

"I appreciate your honesty, Deacon Edwards. Let's agree to disagree. I'm just asking that you give me a chance to execute the vision that God has given me for this spoken word concert. If you let your guard down, God will bless our efforts. I also want to encourage you to bring your family with you on Friday," Pastor Miller told him.

"My family doesn't come to church any more, Pastor. Before you and Lady Vivica arrived here at the church, they had too many bad experiences here and they have declared that they don't plan to come to church ever again."

"Don't give up on them, Deacon Edwards. Vivica never stopped praying for me and look at how blessed we are now. I was a mess back in the day, so I know that if anybody knows how to intercede for others, it's Lady Vivica," Pastor Miller beamed.

"Pastor, I can truly say that Miss Vivica has been a blessing to the young women here at Love of God. She definitely keeps their attention during women's bible study. I overheard her telling the women's class a few weeks ago that "at the name of Jesus every knee will bow and everyone must confess that Jesus is Lord". You don't hear people talking about living right and spending eternity with God anymore," Deacon Edwards added.

"God had to bring me to my knees to get my attention. Ten years ago the doctors said my mom's cancer had spread and they had given up on her. To top things off, I was off work and on disability and we were about to lose our home. I finally had to cry out to God," Pastor Miller confided.

"Are you saying that God turned everything around for you?" Deacon Edwards asked.

"No. What I'm saying is that He turned me around."

Deacon Edwards looked him in the eyes.

"You gave me a lot to think about, Pastor. Thank you. I appreciate you taking the time to meet and talk with me today."

"No problem, Deacon. Is there anything else you'd like to discuss?" Pastor asked.

"No, sir. I'm good. "I'll close us in prayer." Deacon offered.

Pastor Miller closed his eyes as the Deacon began to pray.

"Dear Father of Abraham, Isaac and Jacob. Our wheel in the middle of the wheel. Our great I am and lily of the valley. Our bright and morning star. Our Rose of Sharon. It's me, oh, Lord. Standing in the need of prayer. We thank you for every blessing you have given us. Hear your servant's prayer. In the name of the Father, the Son and the Holy Ghost, thank you and Amen!"

They shook hands and gave one another a quick hug.

"Have a good day, Pastor. See you Friday night."

"See you Friday, Deacon Edwards."

Deacon Edwards picked up his hat and left the pastor's office. Before leaving the church, he checked all the restrooms to make sure they were clean and stocked with paper towels and hand soap. He then checked the kitchen pantry and noted what items needed to be ordered and restocked.

He walked through the sanctuary to ensure it was clean. He picked up candy wrappers and tissues from the pews and floor. He placed bibles in their proper places and then made sure there were bottles of water in the pulpit.

Satisfied that the church was clean and orderly, Deacon Edwards put his hat on his head and walked to his car. His car was almost 20 years old, but it was reliable. He often joked that because he took such good care of his car, his car took good care of him. He turned the ignition and it started immediately. He slowly exited the parking lot. He lived approximately10 miles from the church and he had been actively involved for more than 40 years. He had been appointed as the chairman of the deacon board 15 years earlier and took pride in his role.

After meeting with Deacon Edwards, Pastor Miller was glad to have a few minutes to relax before his next appointment. A young couple had recently contacted him to request premarital counseling from him; he was happy to share some wisdom with them before they exchanged vows. He was known to refuse to perform marriages unless the couple had at least three counseling sessions with him. He believed that marriage was not to be entered into lightly and that marriage was a lifetime commitment.

Pastor Miller was reading a book about millennials and the church when he heard a knock on his door. He put the book back on the bookshelf and opened his door. He smiled broadly as he welcomed the couple and motioned for them to sit down. After counseling with them for a little more than hour, the couple left. Pastor Miller locked the church and headed to his favorite coffeehouse. His guilty pleasure was caramel iced coffee with a few extra pumps of sweet syrup. He ordered his drink and seated himself at a small table near the window that overlooked the main street. He enjoyed his drink while reading a few articles in the local newspaper. He folded the paper and left it on the table for the next customer to read. He walked across the parking lot, unlocked his car and started the engine, but before pulling out of the parking space, he put in his favorite old school gospel song, "He's

Preparing Me", by Daryl Coley. He played that CD several times a week because he loved the lyrics. He often said the song encouraged him. He pulled into his garage at home, just as the song was ending. He turned off the engine and sat in the car for a few moments. He was grateful for the life he had with Vivica. He whispered a prayer of thanksgiving before walking in the house.

As soon as he entered the house, he could hear the undeniable sounds of Boney James' *Sweet Thing* through all the speakers. Vivica was removing turkey wings from the oven just as he walked in.

"The calendar says its Thursday night, but it looks like Sunday dinner in here!" He exclaimed. "What's in these pots?" He asked while lifting the lids on the pots closest to him.

"We've got smothered turkey wings, rice and gravy, cabbage and cornbread. I was hungry," Vivica explained.

"Apparently!" He laughed. I'll go wash my hands and get ready to eat.

"Everything's ready, so I'll set the table," Vivica responded.

Pastor Miller's mother usually had dinner with them, but decided to let them enjoy a quiet and relaxing evening without her.

They ate dinner and danced to a few of their favorite songs, until Pastor Miller stepped on Vivica's foot. They laughed like schoolchildren at his inability to dance. They finally decided to call it a day. They cleared the table, rinsed the dishes and filled the dishwasher before heading upstairs. They knelt beside the bed, joined hands and prayed together. Pastor Miller was snoring as soon as his head hit the pillow. Vivica turned off the light and fell asleep pretty quickly, too.

They slept soundly until the next morning, when Pastor Miller got up to get ready for a monthly Pastor's Community Action meeting. He was dressed and gone before Vivica woke up.

Chapter Five

Pastor Darrelle Brown was sitting at his desk, doing some work on his computer. He was interrupted when someone knocked on his office door.

"Come in."

It was his sister, Simone. "Hey, 'Mookie'. Here's your mail." She immediately started laughing, when she realized she had called him by his childhood nickname. "I'm sorry, Darrelle. I know I agreed not to call you by your nickname while we're working. That slipped. My bad."

"It's all good. Nobody else is here, so no harm, no foul." He assured her.

Simone placed one piece of mail on his desk at a time, glancing at each piece. She scanned a flyer before speaking again. "Pastor Miller, of Love of God Christian Fellowship, has invited us to a fundraiser next Friday night. It's a gospel concert and spoken word event."

Darrelle nodded his head, but he was preoccupied and does not look at her.

"Do we have any conflicts on the calendar that evening?"

she asked him. Darrelle was still focused on what he was doing and didn't respond. She shook her head in despair and walked over to the calendar that was hanging on the wall behind Darrelle's desk and looked at the date. "We don't have anything planned. Do you want me to see if a couple of our young adults are available to perform?" she asked.

"Yes. Please do." He finally responded. "Be sure to reach out to that young lady who joined a few months ago. I can't think of her name, but I believe it starts with a K. I remember her performing a powerful spoken word piece for our talent show." He said.

"Her name is Keenya" His sister told him.

"That's her." He said enthusiastically.

"Apparently she's done something to get your attention. It looks like you're blushing."

"I'd be lying if I said I hadn't noticed how pretty she is, and it's a bonus that she's been faithfully attending worship service and Bible Study. Her big, beautiful dimples are a plus, too." He chuckled.

"You are too much! I'll definitely check with *Lady Dimples* to find out if she is available," Simone replied.

"So, what's up with the fundraiser? What's going on with the church?" He asked.

"I am not one to gossip, but I heard that they are losing the church and that they're trying to raise money to keep it."

"Wow! That's messed up. But, that's what they get. They should have *gave* me that senior pastor position when I interviewed for it."

"First of all, it's should have *given* and God knows your heart and He knows if your motives weren't pure."

"Thank you, Ms. English Professor, for that quick English 101 lesson. How's this? They should have given me that job." He began speaking in a formal matter, pronouncing and enunciating each word correctly. "From the outside it looks like they're doing ok and have plenty of money over there. Have you seen what those members drive? There's nothing but Benzes and Beemers in that parking lot." He lamented.

Simone shook her head in disgust. "God already knew what you wanted to do and I'm sure He wasn't pleased."

Darrelle had a puzzled look on his face. "What do you mean?" He asked her.

"Never mind; don't worry about it," she picked up her cell phone and other belongings from his desk and got ready to leave."

"No, finish what you started. You have never held your tongue. You've been speaking your mind since you were knee-high and you think you're the voice of reason, so speak now or forever hold your peace."

"Darrelle, your actions have been less than honorable since you started pastoring this church a year ago, and the only reason I stay here is to keep an eye on you."

"I don't need you to watch me, ok? I am a grown man and I handle my business. You must have forgotten that I've had your back since we were kids."

"You're right, Darrelle. You have been a great big brother. We argue and fight like all brothers and sisters do, but I've noticed a change in you and it bothers me." She told him.

"Do you realize that I've had to fight for both of us since we were kids? I'm tired of fighting. I'm tired of waiting for things to happen. I'm starting to make things happen!"

"Darrelle, you have to learn to wait on God and be of good courage."

"Apparently God's been busy because, I haven't been able to catch a break lately." He replied.

"I'm not trying to preach to you, but if you delight yourself in the Lord, He will give you the desires of your heart."

"Little sis, you know I love you, right?" Darrelle questioned. "And, I don't know if you're getting these little motivational quotes from that lady who fixes everybody's life or from Dr. Phil, but miss me with all of that, ok?"

"Seriously, Darrelle? Those aren't motivational quotes. I'm quoting scriptures. Wow! And you're my pastor! Lord, help us all," Simone answered.

"Whatever. Do you and I'll do me, ok?" He replied.

"Be careful of how you're living. You'll have to answer to God one day," she responded.

"I've got questions for Him, so I hope He'll be ready to answer to me, too," Darrelle fired back.

She was shocked by her brother's behavior. "Now you've crossed the line and I'm done with this conversation. You just remember that every dog has its day," she scolded.

"Well, I know *that's* not scripture!" he chuckled and shook his head.

"I give up. I'll be at my desk. I'll call Pastor Miller's office to let them know that we'll be there next Friday," she told him.

"Do that, ok? As a matter of fact, when you call him please set up a meeting between the pastor and myself, I'd like to meet him before Friday and see what he's done with the church," he requested.

"What are you up to?" she inquired.

"Nothing. Why?" He asked her.

"I don't like that look in your eyes, Darrelle. I don't even know who you are anymore. You need prayer," she lamented.

"I can't stop you from praying, so do what you do." He snapped.

Simone stared silently at her brother for a few seconds, while clenching her jaw. Realizing their conversation was going nowhere, she hastily left his office and shut the door behind her. She fought back tears as she walked to her cubicle and sat down. She prayed silently for inner peace as she locked her desk. She removed her lunch pail from the overhead cabinet above her desk, picked up her purse and left the church. Her thoughts were scattered as she got in her car and pulled out of the church parking lot. She was concerned about Darrelle.

As soon as Simone left his office, Darrelle got up from his chair and walked over to his office window. He looked up at the sky and took a deep breath. It was late evening and the sun was starting to set. He could see an orange glow on the horizon. This was his favorite time of day. Within a couple of minutes, the sun had set. Darrelle went back to his desk, logged off his laptop, picked up his keys and locked the church before getting in his car and heading toward his apartment. Traffic was unusually heavy, but that didn't bother him. The extra time in the car gave him an opportunity to think about his conversation with Simone. He replayed their conversation over and over in his mind. He knew his sister loved him; he hoped the tension between them would be non-existent when they returned to work the next day.

He was lost in thought when he reached the street where he lived. He was surprised to find a parking spot near his apartment, as street parking in Los Angeles can be challenging. He locked his car and walked a little less than a block to his apartment. When he opened the door to his apartment and stepped inside, he was pleasantly surprised to find that Simone had used the spare key, which he had given her, to let herself in and that she had prepared his favorite dinner: country fried steak, garlic mashed potatoes and sautéed spinach.

Darrelle and Simone engaged in small talk while they ate. Neither one mentioned their earlier argument. After dinner, Darrelle helped Simone clear the table. She offered to wash dishes, but he thanked her and told her that he would wash them. He told her she had done more than enough by preparing dinner.

When Simone was ready to leave, Darrelle walked her to her car and hugged her. He watched her brake lights gradually grow faint as her car disappeared from view.

When he returned to his apartment, Darrelle washed dishes and cleaned the kitchen before taking a warm shower. He knelt beside his bed and prayed. He was relieved to finally get in bed. When he laid his head on his pillow, he smiled when he realized that Simone prepared dinner as a peace offering. Before he drifted off to sleep, he began to think about how fortunate he was to have a sister that loved him despite his faults and shortcomings. As most siblings do, they often had disagreements, but always managed to forgive one another and move on.

Darrelle loved his sister and would do anything to protect her. He regretted that they were separated from one another for so many years while he was in foster care, but he was glad they were reunited after he aged out of the foster care system.

When Simone opened the door to her apartment, she saw her roommate and her roommate's boyfriend curled up together on the couch, sharing a bowl of popcorn and watching a movie. Her roommate told her the movie had just started and told her that she was welcome to join them, but she declined. Simone was emotionally drained and she simply wanted to shower, read her nightly devotional and go to bed.

Before she got in bed, she whispered a prayer for her brother, Darrelle. She was troubled by the way he had been acting. He had been uncharacteristically argumentative lately, so she was happy they quickly made up over dinner.

When she was in her teens, her mother had instilled in her that "food always brings people together". Reconciling with Darrelle tonight was proof her mother's theory was right.

Chapter Six

Vivica had gotten up shortly after Pastor Miller had left, as she planned to do some spring cleaning. She removed the linen from all the beds upstairs and had washed and dried one load after another and remade the beds. Next, she tackled the walk-in closet in the master bedroom. She bagged all of the clothes and shoes that she planned to donate to a local charity. She cleaned both bathrooms and vacuumed the bedrooms before getting undressed to get in the shower, when she heard her daughter, Jaden, yelling to her from downstairs.

"Hello? Is anybody home?" Jaden waited for a response and she could hear the faint sound of her mother coughing.

"Hey, Jaden. I'm getting ready to take a quick shower, but I'll be right down!" Vivica answered.

"Ok," Jaden responded.

Jaden looked down at the stack of mail on the table and began flipping through it. Three envelopes were addressed to her, so she put them in her purse. She went to the kitchen and opened the refrigerator, looking for something to snack on while she waited for her mom to come downstairs. She had just settled in at the dining room table with a bowl of blueberries when her mother entered the room.

"To what do I owe this surprise visit?" Vivica asked.

Jaden put her right hand over her heart and pretended to be hurt that her mother would ask that question.

"Do I have to have a reason to stop by and see my parents?" Jaden asked.

"Look. I know my child. You don't just stop by in the middle of the day for nothing. You're either picking up your mail or you need us to do something. Let's hear it; what's up?" Vivica looked at her daughter.

After a long pause, Jaden finally spoke. "I was answering phones at the church office yesterday morning and I received a call from Pastor Darrelle Brown's secretary."

"Isn't Darrelle Brown the new pastor whose church is down the street from ours?" Vivica asked. She coughed a few times before grabbing a bottle of water from the kitchen.

"Yes, that's him. His secretary said he wanted to set up a meeting with Daddy for today and it was something about that call that made me uneasy," Jaden told her.

"Did she say what the meeting was about?"

"She really wouldn't give me any information. She just said that Pastor Brown wanted to meet with Daddy before the spoken word event on Friday. Have you and daddy met Pastor Brown yet?" Jaden asked.

"Not yet. I've heard that he's fairly young, in his early or mid-twenties, and from what everyone says he is a pretty nice young man."

"I'm not sure about him, but ok," Jaden mumbled.

"You worry too much, young lady. Let it go." Her

mother told her.

"I'm usually a good judge of character and like I said, I got an uneasy feeling while I was talking to her," she added.

"You and that vivid imagination of yours...you get worked up over nothing," Vivica assured her.

"I hope you're right," she exhaled. "I'd better get out of here. I'm meeting up with Leah and Nikki to do a little shopping."

"I thought you said you were broke?" Vivica raised her eyebrows.

"I am, but I was hoping that my beautiful, sweet mother would let me hold some money until my text payday," she responded, while batting her eyelashes at her mother.

"I knew you hadn't stopped by just to say hello! I know you like a book!"

"Seriously, mom. I did stop by to ask you about Pastor Brown and you know I will pay you back!" She promised.

"I've heard that before!" Vivica replied.

Vivica's purse was on the dining room chair, so she reached over to get her wallet and gave Jaden some money. Jaden flashed a big smile, before giving her mom a kiss on the cheek.

"I can't help myself! I love to shop; it's in my DNA! I am my mother's child! I would be willing to bet you've got a couple of new items hidden in your closet that Daddy knows nothing about." Jaden joked as she walked toward the door to leave.

Vivica walked Jaden to the door and gave her daughter a kiss on the cheek and jokingly motioned for Jaden to lower her voice and whispered, "We're not talking about me right now, young lady!

"See there! I knew it! I'm telling Daddy!" Jaden teased while Vivica pushed her out of the door. Jaden got in her car and tapped her horn and waved.

"Be careful, Jaden. Call me later. Love you!" She yelled as Jaden backed out of the driveway.

Shortly after Jaden left, Vivica started yawning, and figured she was tired as a result of the tedious housecleaning she had done. As soon as she went upstairs to take a nap, Pastor Miller called to say he had a dinner meeting and would be home late, so she didn't need to prepare dinner. And, to her surprise, Mother Miller had told her earlier that she would warm some leftovers, so Vivica didn't have to worry about her. She had a free day.

She didn't realize she had slept as long as she did, until Pastor Miller kissed her on the cheek and woke her up when he got home at 9 PM.

He encouraged her to put on her pajamas and get in bed, and she complied without any resistance.

She took a warm shower, put on her pajamas and snuggled in close to Pastor Miller. He was already snoring. She whispered a prayer and soon fell asleep. She loved her life.

Chapter Seven

Darrelle Brown pulled into the empty parking lot of Love of God Christian Fellowship. He parked and turned off the ignition. He sat in the car for a couple of minutes before getting out and entering the double glass doors leading into the church lobby.

He took a deep breath before opening the doors and walking in the lobby. He was impressed with the open floor plan and contemporary look. To his right was a lounge area with café tables, chairs and an overstuffed couch. To the left was a bookstore and small coffee shop.

"Boy, oh, boy. What I could've did, I mean 'what I could have *done* with this church." Darrelle's thoughts were interrupted when Pastor Miller walked in.

"Pastor Brown, it's nice to finally meet you," Pastor Miller said, while extending his right hand.

"Its nice meeting you, too, but please call me Darrelle."

"Darrelle, it is. My office is right down the hall. Follow me."

As they passed by the sanctuary, Darrelle noticed that

the wooden pews had been removed and replaced by rows of plush and comfortable chairs. A clear acrylic pulpit now stood where the oak one had been.

Darrelle was finding it difficult to hide his jealousy. His small church was struggling to keep the lights on each week and it was apparent that wasn't the case here at Love of God Christian Fellowship church. Everything was modern and new.

Pastor Miller motioned for Darrelle to sit down when they entered his office.

"Would you like some coffee or water?" He asked Darrelle.

"No, thank you. I'm good, Pastor."

Pastor Miller spoke as he poured himself a cup of coffee. "I was happy to hear that you and your congregation accepted our invitation to come to our spoken word concert this Friday night. Thank you for saying yes," Pastor Miller said.

"We are looking forward to fellowshipping with you," Darrelle replied.

"I am, too, Darrelle, and I'm glad you decided to stop by." Pastor Miller took a seat behind his desk. "I hear we have a few things in common."

"Oh, really? What is that?" Darrelle inquired.

"I was told that you have only been pastoring for about a year or so, and I was elected to pastor here just about a year ago myself," Pastor Miller shared.

"Yes, sir. That's correct. I opened the doors to Jubilee Christian Center a little more than 10 months ago."

"That's impressive and I commend you, because at your age church was the furthest thing from my mind," Pastor

Miller added.

"If you had been through what I've been through, you would have to believe that there's a God or you'd go crazy," Darrelle inhaled and slowly exhaled.

"It sounds like you've had some hardships. If you don't mind me asking, did you have a tough childhood?" Pastor Miller pried.

"*Tough* is an understatement, Pastor. My sister and I were in and out of foster care until we were 18. Let me clarify that. I was in and out of foster care. My sister was fortunate enough to get adopted when she was 4 or 5 years old."

"I'm sorry to hear that," Pastor Miller spoke quietly.

"It's ok. What doesn't kill you makes you stronger, right?" Darrelle answered.

"That's what I hear," Pastor Miller assured him.

Darrelle inhaled and exhaled. "I just wanted to come over and introduce myself since we hadn't had a chance to meet yet. I was glad to receive the invitation to the concert this weekend, but I wanted to come by and tell you myself that if you ever need anything, don't hesitate to call. Here's my card." Darrelle handed him a business card as he stood to leave.

"That's nice of you, Darrelle. I've been in California most of my adult life and I'm always surprised when someone goes out of their way to show kindness like this. I appreciate that."

"Oh, I'm not from California, Pastor. I'm from Mississippi. Actually, I was born in Alabama and raised in Mississippi.

"That explains it. You've got southern hospitality."

Pastor Miller chuckled. "My wife and I are from Alabama, too. I'm from Montgomery and my wife is from a little a little blip on the map: Cardiff, Alabama."

"Seriously? If I'm not mistaken, Cardiff is where I was born," Darrelle told him.

"Every day I'm convinced of how small the world is. I'd be willing to bet that my wife knows your people," Pastor Miller said.

"I've never met anyone else from Cardiff. Is your wife here? I'd love to meet her." It was apparent that Darrelle was excited about the prospect of meeting someone from his hometown.

"No, she's not here right now, but I'll make sure you meet her on Friday night," Pastor Miller promised.

"You have no idea how excited I am to meet someone from back home," Darrelle confided. "We moved from Cardiff when my sister and I were really young so I don't remember too much about it."

"According to my wife, there's not much to Cardiff, so I don't think you missed much," Pastor Miller joked.

"That's what I've heard," Darrelle laughed. "Anyway, I've taken up enough of your time, Pastor Miller. It was nice meeting you."

"It was nice meeting you, as well. Please feel free to bring as many of your family and friends as you'd like on Friday night. I want to pack the church and show support to the young adults who will be performing."

"I mentioned it during Bible Study last week and a couple of our young adults want to perform. I will confirm that they signed up and I'll let your secretary know. I'm also thinking about doing one of my original spoken word pieces, too," Darrelle added.

"I appreciate your support!" Pastor Miller responded enthusiastically.

"You're welcome. We're happy to help. See you Friday," Darrelle responded and shook hands with Pastor Miller before leaving the office.

Pastor Miller sat down at his desk and started reading emails. He had some free time before his next appointment.

Chapter Eight

It was Friday night and the sanctuary of Love of God Christian Fellowship was very noisy with chatter and lively conversations, as guests began arriving for the spoken word concert, which had actually morphed into a talent show. All those who were scheduled to perform were ushered into the multipurpose room, located just off the main sanctuary. Each performer was greeted by Vivica, as she gave final instructions and answered any questions they may have had. Content that everyone was ready, she poked her head in the sanctuary. She was thrilled that so many had responded to the invitation to attend. She preferred to work behind-the-scenes and she always did a great job coordinating large events.

Vivica was well-spoken and very comfortable addressing large crowds, so she had volunteered to emcee the concert. After answering all questions and making sure every detail had been taken care of, she asked everyone to gather in a circle and join hands for prayer. After leading the group of performers in prayer, she wished them well and then exited the multipurpose room and walked into the sanctuary. Everyone began to quiet down when they saw her enter.

Vivica pressed her shoulders back as she confidently approached the podium and carefully removed the microphone from the stand and greeted the crowd. "Praise the Lord, everybody!" Everyone shouted, "Praise the Lord," in response.

"Good evening, and welcome to the Love of God Christian Fellowship," she continued. "I am Vivica Miller and on behalf of Pastor James Miller and all of our faithful members here, we welcome you. We know that you could have spent your Friday evening anywhere you desired, so we're grateful that you're here with us."

After reminding everyone to put their cell phones on silent mode, Vivica then ensured everyone had received a donation envelope and gently reiterated that the concert was a fundraiser. She introduced the performers for the first half of the program and then she sat on the front pew with her husband, and special guests and dignitaries from the community. Inspirational music, spirited dance routines, spoken word and singing filled the sanctuary for just about two hours.

The final performance of the evening was a rousing gospel mime performance, which received a standing ovation. What an evening!

Vivica accompanied Pastor Miller to the microphone and smiled as her husband thanked everyone for their support.

"We thank each of you for coming tonight and we thank you for your generosity," Pastor Miller began. "Your love and support have been very encouraging, but equally important, I'm happy to announce that thanks to you, the total pledges and offering received tonight was more than double the amount we needed! We will not lose Love of God Christian Fellowship to foreclosure! Glory to God!" His announcement was met with thunderous cheers and applause.

He continued, "If there is nothing more, please stand and join hands with the person next to you.

Father, we thank You for Your daily provisions and for Your everlasting love. We ask now that You continue to bless us collectively and individually and give us traveling grace as we go our separate ways. Continue to watch over us and keep us. It's in the name of Your Son that I humbly pray. Amen and amen!

The guests mingled for a few minutes and then the crowd started to disperse.

Pastor Miller and Vivica stood at the back door of the church shaking hands with everyone and thanking them for their support and attendance. The sanctuary was practically empty, except for two or three guests, when Pastor Miller saw Pastor Darrelle Brown approaching. Darrelle was accompanied by a young lady and he didn't show any emotion when he shook Pastor Miller's hand. "Darrelle, I didn't know you were so talented! That spoken word piece that you performed was amazing!"

"Thank you, Pastor Miller," he responded dryly. He added, "I'd like for you to meet my sister, Simone." Simone extended her hand to shake hands with both Pastor Miller and Vivica Miller.

"It's very nice to meet you, Simone," the Millers said in unison while shaking Simone's hand.

"My pleasure," She responded.

"I'm Pastor Miller and this is my beautiful wife who keeps me grounded, Lady Vivica Miller." Pastor Miller smiled.

Vivica extended her hand to shake Darrelle's hand, but he kept his hands in his pockets, which caused a moment of awkward silence.

"Well, well, well. I finally get to meet the infamous Vivica Miller," Darrelle finally spoke. "I've heard so much about you."

"I hope it was all good," Vivica stammered.

"It depends," Darrelle responded curtly.

"Excuse me?" Vivica replied.

"I said it depends!" Darrelle raised his voice.

Jaden overheard the commotion and quickly finished the conversation she was having with one of the performers and swiftly came and stood next to her father.

"Daddy, is everything ok?" she inquired.

"I'm not sure what's going on, Jaden. I'm trying to figure it out."

"Darrelle, what's wrong with you? You're being disrespectful!" Pastor Miller said. "What is your problem?"

"Ask your wife," Darrelle replied.

Vivica was momentarily stunned by Darrelle's response, but she finally replied, "I have no idea what this is about, James."

"Darrelle, do you know my wife?" Pastor Miller asked.

"The better question is *does your wife know us*?" he responded, while pointing to himself and Simone.

"What does that even mean?" Pastor Miller asked. He looked at Vivica and asked, "Do you know him?"

"This is the first time I've met him!" she snapped. "Pastor Brown, what is this about?"

"Well, let's see if this refreshes your memory, Miss Vivica," Darrelle began.

"Cardiff, Alabama, January, 1988. Two little kids ages 6 and 3, were left in an apartment by themselves for days with no electricity and no food, by their mom who was addicted to crack. Those kids clung to one another because they were scared of the dark. Shall I continue?" He asked, and continued before Vivica could respond. "Those two kids have been searching for their mother since that day. Is it becoming clear to you yet, Miss Vivica? Simone and I are the kids you left behind!"

Simone screamed and almost collapsed before she ran from the sanctuary. Darrelle ran after her and caught up with her in the church lobby. He held her while she sobbed uncontrollably.

Vivica covered her mouth. She was in shock. Pastor Miller and Jaden stared at her.

"Mom, how could you?" Jaden finally asked, while tears rolled down her cheeks.

"I was a different person back then," she responded and reached out to console her daughter.

Jaden pulled away. "Don't touch me! Don't you dare touch me!" She responded angrily before folding her arms across her stomach and doubling over until she almost fell.

Vivica turned to face Pastor Miller and then reached out with one hand to touch his arm. He pulled his arm away without saying anything. He turned his attention to Jaden, who was sobbing loudly. He put his arm around Jaden's shoulders and tried to get her to stand up straight. He then led her out of the sanctuary, leaving Vivica behind. Alone.

Vivica fell to her knees and screamed in agony. With her fists clenched and pressed to her forehead, she sobbed uncontrollably for several minutes. She finally got up from the floor and slowly left the sanctuary. She sat quietly in her car for a few minutes before turning the ignition.

The drive home seemed to take longer than usual. She had many thoughts racing through her mind. The most pressing thought was whether her husband and daughter would be able to forgive her or not. She pulled her car in the garage, turned off the ignition and got out of the car. The house was dark when she walked in. Pastor Miller's car was in the garage, so she was glad to know he was home. What could she say to make him understand why she did what she did?

As soon as she walked in the house, she turned on the lamp and she was startled to see Pastor Miller sitting in the dark, with a blank look on his face.

"James, you almost gave me a heart attack!" Why are you sitting here in the dark?" she asked.

He didn't respond.

"James, you and I have weathered some storms and I know we can get through this," she continued.

Pastor Miller continued staring blankly into space.

"We need to talk about this and…"

"Save it, Vivica! Pastor Miller interrupted her before she could finish her statement.

"Can you please just give me a moment to explain?" she pleaded.

"There's nothing to explain!" he snapped. "You can pack your bags and leave! We are done!"

Their conversation was interrupted by a knock at the door.

"I don't want to talk to anybody. I'm going upstairs," Vivica said and left the room.

Pastor Miller opened the door and he was surprised to see Darrelle.

"Come on in."

"Pastor, I just wanted to come by and apologize for what happened," Darrelle offered.

"There's no need for you to apologize. I'm just disappointed that I found out the way I did." Pastor Miller replied.

"Please understand that I never intended to hurt anybody, but when I finally tracked down Vivica and found out where she was, I couldn't get past the fact that she never even came to look for us. It's like we didn't exist to her," Darrelle quietly responded.

"I'm trying to get my head around this whole thing. I'm not even sure how to move forward at this point," Pastor Miller admitted.

"Simone and I are still really confused. Simone wants to get to know Vivica, but I'm not sure how I feel. I just need to hear her tell me she's sorry or to tell me why she left us and never looked for us," Darrelle's voice quivered.

"I'm at a loss as to what to say to you. I can only say we all have to be led by God and not by our emotions," Pastor Miller said in an attempt to encourage Darrelle and himself.

Darrelle inhaled deeply. "As hard as it, I know I need to take your advice. Again, I'm sorry for how this has turned out. I just couldn't let another day go by without saying something and making her face us. It was killing me."

"I understand, Darrelle. There are no hard feelings." Pastor Miller extended his right hand to shake hands with Darrelle, but after a momentary hesitation, Darrelle hugged him instead.

"I need to go and check on Simone. Thanks for hearing me out, Pastor," he said as he opened the door to leave.

"You're welcome, Darrelle. Take care of yourself."

Pastor Miller quietly closed the door when Darrelle left and sat down in his recliner. After a few minutes of silence, there was another knock at the door. Pastor Miller opened the door and it was Deacon Edwards. He invited the deacon in and offered him a seat.

"Pastor, I just wanted to come by and check on you." Deacon Edwards said.

"I appreciate it, Deacon Edwards. I'm doing ok." He barely spoke above a whisper.

"I'm here on behalf of our Board of Directors and we all want you to know we're here for you and Lady Vivica."

"I appreciate that. I really do. Why don't you get the Board together tomorrow night so I can come and talk with them? Sister Vivica and I are probably going to separate for a while and figure out what we want to do and go from there. I want to prepare the Board."

"Now, now, now, hold on Pastor," Deacon Edwards stuttered. "Not so fast. I don't know what to say. Have you considered marriage counseling? My brother is a licensed marriage and family counselor. Here's his card." He said as he handed Pastor Miller a business card.

"I forgot your brother was a marriage counselor. I'll think it over and let you know if I decide to call him. I'm not sure that he can help, but I'll give it some thought."

"Alright, that sounds good. I just wanted to stop by and check on you. I don't want to keep you. I'll call the Board members as soon as I get home." He said and turned to leave. He was almost to the door, but he stopped and turned back to Pastor Miller.

"By the way, my family came to the program and they really enjoyed it. I'm sorry you didn't get a chance to meet them. They said they'll come back on Sunday for church service."

"That is so good to hear. It amazes me that when things seem out of control, God reminds us that He's always in control, no matter what." Pastor Miller smiled slightly.

"I'm sorry about what you and your family are going through, Pastor, but one thing I learned from Sis. Vivica is that prayer not only changes things, prayer changes people. I remember you telling me that she never gave up on you before you came to the Lord. I'm going to leave that right there for you to think about, Pastor."

"Thank you for that reminder, Deacon Edwards. See you at the meeting tomorrow night."

"See you tomorrow, Pastor." Deacon Edwards turned the doorknob to leave, but didn't open the door. He turned toward Pastor again. "Pastor, I feel led to pray for you and your family, if you don't mind."

Pastor Miller smiled.

Deacon Edwards placed his hands on the pastor's shoulders and began praying.

"Dear Father of Abraham, Isaac and Jacob, Our Wheel in the Middle of the Wheel, The Great I Am, Our Lily of the Valley, and Bright and Morning Star, our Rose of Sharon. It's me Oh Lord, standing in the need of prayer." There was a shift in the Deacon's

prayer; he slowed down a bit and changed the tone of his prayer. He was quiet for moment and then he continued. "Actually, Lord, I'm standing before you on behalf of my pastor and his wife. Guide them and give them clarity of mind to make decisions that honor you. Order their steps and encourage their hearts today. In Your Name, please hear your humble servant's prayer. Amen!"

Pastor Miller and Deacon Edwards hugged for a brief moment before Deacon Edwards picked up his hat and opened the door.

"Good night, Pastor." Deacon Edwards said quietly as he was leaving.

"Good night, Deacon. Thank you again for coming by."

"You're welcome." He responded.

Pastor Miller closed the door and spoke out loud, "Lord, you've never let me down before. I'm going to take you at your Word to not put more on me than I can bear. Amen."

As soon as he finished praying, Vivica cleared her throat to let him know that she was in the room. She had two rolling suitcases with her.

"If you're not expecting anybody else, I'd like to pick up where we left off." Vivica told him.

"Vivica, I don't think you understand. I don't have anything to say to you. I need some space right now."

"Come on, James. We've been married over 30 years. We've always talked openly about everything. I need you to listen. Please just hear me out." She pleaded with him.

Pastor Miller looked at his cellphone and turned on the timer. "You've got three minutes, Vivica, and the clock is ticking."

She coughed before she spoke. "When I met you, I couldn't believe that God had answered my prayers, by sending such a good man to love me. I had been sober for a little more than a year when we met and because things were so good between us, I couldn't bring myself to tell you about my past." She stared downward after she spoke.

"Do you realize what you've done? You and I counsel young couples and advise them to be honest with one another. We have warned every couple to be honest with one another, because lies will eventually hurt their marriage. Our entire marriage has been one big lie! How could you do this to me? How could you do this to us?" He raised his voice.

"I'm so sorry. It never seemed like the right time to tell you about my past and about my children." Vivica cried.

"In more than 30 years of marriage you couldn't find the right time to tell me that you had two kids? Do you know how ridiculous that sounds?" He asked her.

Vivica reached out to touch his arm, but he pulled away. "I never expected Darrelle and Simone to find me. I am so sorry. We all need time to process this." She told him.

"Did you hear what you just said? *You didn't expect them to find you?* You can't be serious!" He raised his voice again. "I don't need time to process anything, Vivica. Your three minutes are up. I'll have my attorney contact you." He spoke sternly.

"James, would you please just..." She started to reason with him, but James interrupted her again before she could finish speaking. "I don't have to do anything except live my life. We don't have anything else to talk about. You can leave now." He pointed to the door. "Now!" He shouted.

Vivica turned away from him and she started to walk away. She stopped in her tracks and shook her head back and forth. She walked back over to where Pastor Miller was standing and stood less than a foot away from him.

"Let me tell you something, James Lee Miller. In the 30 years that we've been married, I have never raised my voice at you. I have never disrespected you and I have loved you more than I've loved myself at times, but please hear me and hear me real good on this. This is my house, too, and I'm not leaving. Now if you don't want to sit down and talk this out like we're civilized adults and if you don't want to be under the same roof with me, YOU can leave…and you can take your mama with you."

Pastor Miller's mother could be heard clearing her throat from the family room. They had both forgotten she was in the house.

"These walls are paper thin, Vivica. Watch yourself." Mother Miller warned.

Pastor Miller lowered his voice before speaking. "Vivica, I'm warning you. I have been as patient as I can be. I'm asking you nicely to leave."

"And I'm telling you nicely that I'm not going anywhere."

Pastor Miller stared at Vivica, but doesn't say anything.

She stared back at him and raised her eyebrows. She then folded her arms across her chest. "I guess we're at an impasse." She gloated.

"I guess we are," he responded.

"My suitcases and I will be upstairs. Good night, Reverend." Vivica stood on her tiptoes and kissed him on the cheek and turned and walked away, pulling the two suitcases behind her.

Pastor Miller was astonished by his wife's behavior and couldn't believe she had the audacity to kiss him on the cheek. He instinctively started laughing deviously as she was walking away. "You don't know who you're messing with, Vivica! You must've forgotten that I haven't been a pastor all my life!" He said loud enough for her to hear.

"That woman has lost her mind." He spoke out loud, to himself, before walking over to the hall closet to get a couple of blankets and a pillow. He decided to sleep on the couch.

Chapter Nine

Early the next morning, Vivica was sitting at the kitchen table, drinking coffee, when Pastor Miller entered the kitchen. He looked at her and shook his head, but didn't say anything to her. He reached for the coffee decanter and filled his coffee thermos and then turned to leave the kitchen. Vivica stood up to confront him.

"Good morning, James. I'm sure you didn't see me sitting here or are you ignoring me?" She asked.

"Vivica, I'm not in the mood for your drama, OK? Not today." He responded.

"Let's sit down and talk this out." She continued.

"The only thing I want out is you!" He shouted.

"Alright, Mr. Tough Guy." She responded sarcastically.

Pastor Miller took a few steps closer to her. "Do you think this is a freakin' joke? You are playing with fire." He warned her.

"Is that a threat?" She asked him.

It's a fact and I'm going to leave before it becomes a threat."

"Suit yourself." She said and stepped aside to let him exit the kitchen. Shortly after she sat back down at the table, she heard the electric garage door lift to open and then lower a few seconds later, as it closed, when Pastor Miller left.

A few minutes after he left, she heard a succession of loud knocks at the front door. She walked briskly to the door and opened it. She was surprised to see her daughter, Jaden.

"Come on in, baby." Vivica told her, as she opened the door wider to let Jaden enter. "You should've used your key. Have a seat." She told her between coughs.

Jaden folded across her chest and stood quietly before responding. "I'll stand, thank you."

"OK. So, what's going on with you?" Vivica asked as she sat on the couch.

"Are you really asking me "what's going on"? How could you do this to Daddy? How could you do this to our family? You've got two other kids that you never said anything about! Really?" Jaden shouted.

"Wait just a minute, Jaden. I can't do anything to change my past, but I need you to understand that this doesn't change our relationship." Vivica replied.

"You cannot be serious! I just found out that I've got a sister and a brother and you're telling me this doesn't change our relationship?" Jaden continued yelling.

Vivica reached out to touch Jaden's hand, but Jaden snatched away.

"Don't you dare touch me! I swear I don't know who you are!" She responded.

Vivica forcefully grabbed Jaden's and spoke to her with authority, while enunciating each word. "I'm your mother. That's who I am!"

"No, ma'am! As far as I'm concerned you're just the woman who gave birth to me!" Jaden responded, while snatching her arm from her mother's grip.

Vivica raised her hand, prepared to slap Jaden, but Jaden doesn't flinch. Vivica lowered her hand to her side, and balled it into a fist.

"Listen here, Jaden Chanel Miller. I have given you everything you've ever asked for. You've never had to ask for anything twice. Your dad and I pay most of your bills and, as a matter of fact, we're paying for that apartment you're living in and we pay the note and insurance on that cute little red Mustang that you're driving, so don't you dare stand here and tell me that I'm just the woman who gave birth to you." She spoke sternly.

"You probably did all that out of guilt for what you did to your other kids!" Jaden snapped back.

"I did it because I love you!" Vivica told her emphatically.

"All my life you've told me to be aware of how I carry myself, because I represent God and I represent our family. Was that rule only for me?" She asked.

"Look, I'm not proud of the life I lived before I met your father. I was a different person back then. When I finally got clean, I never looked back." Vivica answered quietly.

"You never looked back? Jaden screamed. "You left two kids behind! That's not ok!"

"I know that, Jaden, but I can't change what I did. I was an addict and I wasn't myself back then," Vivica answered angrily.

Mother Miller entered the room.

"Vivica! Jaden! I can hear you two screaming from my

room. All this yelling isn't necessary." She spoke calmly.

"I'm sorry, Granny, but I get sick of people blaming addiction as an excuse when they hurt others." Jaden responded quietly to her Grandmother.

"Until you've walked a mile in my shoes, little girl, don't judge me. Only God can judge me. We've all sinned and missed the mark".

"Save the sermon for yourself. I think you need it more than I do. I'm good. I don't even know why I came over here!" Jaden said as she walked toward the door.

"Don't you walk out of here, Jaden!" Vivica demanded.

Jaden looks at her mother and shakes her head and then walks over to her Grandmother.

"Bye, Granny." She kissed Mother Miller and gave her a hug.

"Jaden, baby, please don't leave. Let's sit down and talk this out." Mother Miller pleaded.

"I have nothing else to say to her. She's dead to me." Jaden said, while looking at her mother.

"Watch your mouth, Jaden or... " Vivica stopped mid-sentence.

"Or what?" Jaden walked over to Vivica and stood face-to-face to her and repeated the question. "Or what?"

"Jaden, it's probably best that that you go ahead and leave now before I do or say something I'll regret." Vivica said and walked away.

"My pleasure. You have already gotten rid of two other kids, what's one more?" She answered sarcastically.

"Get out! Vivica shouted. "Get out now!"

"Gladly. Bye, Granny." Jaden glanced at her mother as she walked toward the door.

"Bye, baby." Mother Miller said sadly.

Jaden slammed the door behind her.

Vivica and Mother Miller stare at one another momentarily.

"Whatever you're thinking about saying to me, you need to keep it to yourself, OK? I don't want to hear it!" Vivica warned the elder Mrs. Miller.

"Vivica, I know you and I have had our share of problems, but what you don't need is for me to be your enemy." Mrs. Miller said matter-of-factly.

"You don't scare me, old lady."

"I'm not trying to scare you, Vivica. You need to only fear God."

Vivica had a coughing spell and it took her a moment to catch her breath before she could respond.

"Oh, here we go. Do you really have to bring God into everything? I need to get out of here. I've got things to do. I'll get my purse and I'm out." Vivica said.

"Don't let me stop you. I've got things to do myself. I'm cleaning house today." Mother Miller told her.

"You lead such an exciting life!" She responded sarcastically.

"Don't worry about me, sweetheart. Your family is in turmoil. How about you focus your attention there?" Mother Miller told her.

"I'm not worrying about anybody but myself at this point. I've apologized and I'm moving on. If everybody wants to keep holding my past over my head, they can all go straight to…"

"Vivica! What has gotten into you?" Mother Miller interrupted before she could finish her statement.

"Nothing. I'm just sick of all you self-righteous people acting like you've never made a mistake."

"Vivica, you abandoned two kids. That's not a little mistake."

"Mind your business, OK? You don't know anything about my situation." Vivica responded.

"Before you get too spiritual and try to lay hands on me or pray for me, I'm leaving. I'm going shopping," Vivica said.

"Do what you need to do." Mother Miller answered.

Vivica got her purse and keys and walked out.

Mother Miller started pacing back and forth.

Mother Miller went to her bedroom and came back with a small vial of anointing oil. She methodically dabbed a little oil on her finger and then touched the surfaces of every item in the living room: the couch, the tables, the T.V., the lamps.

She began praying out loud, with fervency.

"God, I'm thankful for another opportunity to have a little talk with you. In Hebrews 5:16, it says, "Let us therefore come boldly unto the throne of grace, that we may obtain mercy and find grace to help in time of need", and that's what I'm doing. The forces of evil are trying to destroy the life and the ministry that James and Vivica have built together. Lord, I'm asking you to restore everything that has been taken. Restore their joy, peace and unity today. Rekindle their love and strengthen their bond of commitment to you and to one another. It is my sincere request to have you move like never before. I decree and declare full restoration. I trust you and I thank you. Amen!"

When Mother Miller finished praying, she headed into the kitchen to figure out what she would prepare for dinner.

She always told her family 'good food brings people together".

She looked in the freezer and took out a package of chicken breasts and set them in cold water to thaw out. James liked her oven baked barbequed chicken, so that's what she would prepare, along with some mashed potatoes and her signature okra, corn and tomato succotash.

While the food was cooking, she set the table with the fine china they used for guests and special occasions. She was expecting the night to be special. She had prayed and believed God would answer.

Vivica usually did all of the cooking, so Mother Miller was happy to get a chance to cook. It had been a while.

It was almost 6:00 P.M when Vivica returned home. She didn't say anything to Mother Miller when she walked in. She went to her room.

Pastor Miller arrived home approximately an hour after Vivica arrived. As soon as he walked in, Mother Miller met him at the door.

"Son, I cooked a nice, home-cooked meal for you and Vivica." She told him.

"I'm sorry, Mom. I'm not hungry. I just want to take a shower, do some reading and go to bed." He responded to her.

"I understand, James." Mother Miller responded sullenly.

Pastor Miller considered sleeping on the couch again, but he headed to Jaden's old room and shut the door behind him.

Vivica never came back downstairs. Mother Miller ate dinner by herself.

When she was finished eating, she cleared the table and put the leftover food into storage containers, and placed them in the refrigerator.

She cleaned the kitchen and finally went to her room to take a bath and prepare for bed. She filled the tub with warm water and a floral scented bubble bath. She soaked in the tub for a few minutes and tried to relax, but anxiety got the best of her. She was disappointed that the night didn't go as she thought it would.

When she got out of the tub, she put on a matching gown and robe and sat on the side of her bed and read a few passages from the Book of Psalms. She always felt encouraged and hopeful when she meditated on Bible scriptures. She closed her Bible and returned it to the nightstand. She slowly knelt beside her bed and prayed, asking God to watch over her family and to bring reconciliation and peace.

It took her a few seconds to get from her knees and onto her feet, but when she did, she turned down the comforter and sheets, got in bed and leaned over and turned off the lamp beside her bed. Before she fell asleep, she laid awake for a few minutes thinking about the chaos earlier between Vivica and James and between Vivica and Jaden. She drifted off to sleep, strongly believing everything would be fine.

Chapter Ten

After a restless night of tossing and turning, Pastor Miller slowly got out of bed at 7:15 the next morning. He sat on the side of the bed for a couple of minutes. His thoughts were racing. His family was in turmoil, and that saddened him. He shaved, showered, got dressed and left the house before Vivica and Mother Miller woke up. He backed out of the garage and onto the tree-lined cul-de-sac street that he and Vivica fell in love with when the realtor invited them to an open house 22 years earlier.

He pulled into the parking lot of the nearby corner café to have breakfast. To his surprise, the café was already bustling with several patrons. A few of them looked in his direction and smiled or nodded when he walked in. The atmosphere of the café was always warm and welcoming. A hostess seated him in a corner booth and gave him a menu. He placed his order and looked around the café. Seeing families with small children made him reminisce about when Jaden was younger. He and Vivica used to have breakfast at this cafe every Saturday morning. His thoughts were interrupted when the alarm on his phone beeped to remind him of the meeting that he scheduled with his Board of Directors. He had to eat quickly or risk being late to the meeting.

Traffic was unusually heavy when he left the café. Fortunately, he didn't have far to drive. He parked his car and rushed to the church's conference room. Everyone was quietly talking among themselves.

When Deacon Edwards saw that Pastor Miller had arrived, he called everyone to order.

"Alright, everybody. Pastor's here, so let's give him our attention."

"Thank you, Deacon Edwards. Good morning, everybody." Pastor Miller greeted everyone.

Everyone responded in unison to his greeting.

"I wanted to come and talk to you before you started hearing rumors about Sis. Vivica and myself." He added.

"Pastor, I'm sure you know how quickly bad news spreads. People across town are already calling me and texting to say that they heard there was a fight here at the church." Robyn chimed in.

"That's a doggone shame. People need to pray more and talk less." Mother Miller added.

"Unfortunately, we don't have any control over what people say, but I want you all to know what happened and I want you to hear it directly from me." Pastor Miller said.

"Pastor, you don't owe us any explanation about your personal life." Marva Campbell assured him.

"I realize that, but I'd rather be upfront and honest with you, so that you'll know how to respond to people, if necessary." Pastor Miller responded.

"I understand, Pastor." Marva Campbell told him.

"Let me cut to the chase. As you may have heard by now, before Sis. Vivica and I met, she had already had two kids that I knew nothing about, and they showed up at the program last night and confronted her."

"So, are you saying there actually was a fight?" Robyn questioned.

"No, it wasn't a fight. It was a loud confrontation. Vivica hadn't seen them in almost 35 years," he replied.

"Wow. And they brought that mess here to the church? They're lucky I didn't hear them disrespecting my first lady. It wouldn't have gone down like that. Not on my watch," Robyn said, while rolling up the sleeves on her blouse.

"No, none of us needed to be involved in what happened yesterday. It could've gotten real ugly," Mother Miller added.

"Pastor, what can we do for you and Sis. Vivica?" Miss Marva asked.

"Well, it hurts me to say this, but Sis. Vivica and I are likely going to separate until we can sort things out." Pastor responded.

"Pastor, whatever you do, please don't make any hasty decisions." Marva Campbell replied.

"It wasn't a hasty or easy decision, Miss Marva, but I believe it's best for now. This separation will give us a chance to cool our heads and figure out what we're going to do." Pastor told her.

Robyn shook her head in disappointment.

"Pastor, like I told you last night, you and first lady have our full support." Deacon Edwards added.

"That means a lot, Deacon Edwards. Thank you." Pastor

Miller exhaled loudly before continuing. "That's all I had to share. Does anybody have any questions?"

"Pastor, thank you for letting us know what's going on." Marva Campbell told him.

"Each of you has been very supportive of my family since we arrived, and I appreciate your kindness. Please keep us in prayer as we work through this." He requested.

"We've got your back, Pastor." Robyn responded.

"Alright, if there's nothing else, we can stand and dismiss in prayer. I need to finish preparing my sermon for tomorrow."

As everyone began to stand, Vivica walked in.

"Well, well, well. What do we have here?" Vivica snidely asked. Nobody responded, but she continued. "It looks like some secret little meeting that I wasn't invited to."

"I was meeting with my board so that I could nip any rumors in the bud, concerning last night's commotion." Pastor Miller responded.

"Do you really expect me to believe that's what this meeting is about?" Vivica asked.

"I really don't have to answer to you, but yes, that's what this meeting was about." Pastor Miller told her.

"I do hope you're telling the truth, because if any of you think for a minute that I'm stepping down as first lady, you'd better think again." She warned.

"You don't step down from being a first lady, Vivica. You get replaced by a new first lady!" Mother Miller responded quickly.

Vivica chuckled at Mother Miller's response.

"Trust and believe that being replaced is not even up for debate. I'll burn this church down before I let that happen."

"Don't let your mouth write a check that you may not be able to cover, Vivica. You wouldn't be the first lady if you weren't married to my son. You're where you are because of him, so don't you forget that."

"And your son wouldn't be where he is if it wasn't for me. I've been the one praying and interceding for God to elevate him and bless this church."

"OK, Vivica! That's enough! It's one thing for you to be disrespectful in our home. I'm not going to allow you to disrespect this church." Pastor Miller raised his voice.
"What are you going to do to stop me, James?" She asked.

Pastor Miller stared at her, but didn't say anything.

"That's what I thought." Vivica finally spoke, while trying to suppress a cough.

Deacon Edwards stepped between Pastor Miller and Vivica and pleaded with her.

"Ms. Vivica, don't do this here, ok? You and pastor need to talk privately."

"Why, Deacon Edwards? We're all family here. We don't have any secrets because I'm sure Pastor told you that I had been on drugs at one time and I had two kids out of wedlock, that I abandoned. Why do we need to talk in private now?" She shouted.

"Well, Pastor hadn't said anything about you being on drugs or abandoning your kids. This is some reality TV mess right there." Robyn said, interrupting Vivica's tirade.

"I really didn't think it was necessary to air all our dirty laundry." Pastor Miller said to Vivica.

"Even through all this, James is trying to save your reputation, Vivica. You should be thankful, instead of being so angry." Mother Miller added.

Vivica turned her attention from James and walked over to Mother Miller and got in Mother Miller's face.

"I thought I told you to mind your business earlier. I didn't ask for your opinion!" Vivica shouted.

Mother Miller took a few steps back and took off her earrings.

"I see I'm going to need to lay hands on you today, Vivica." Mother Miller lunged toward Vivica, but Robyn grabbed Mother Miller and pulled her back before she reached Vivica.

Everybody was shocked by Vivica's behavior, but even more shocked by Mother Miller's actions.

"Mom! What are you doing?" Pastor Miller yelled before he stepped between his wife and mother.

"I apologize, son. I've had all I can take of her being so rude and mean." Mother Miller humbly apologized.

"Mom, have a seat and let me handle this." He told her before turning back to address Vivica.

"Vivica, please leave now! He shouted.

Before Vivica turned to leave, she acted like she was going to lunge at Mother Miller.

"Come on, Ms. Vivica." Deacon Edwards gently guided Vivica toward the door. "Let's go before this gets out of hand."

"I'll leave, but make sure you understand what I said. I'm not stepping down and I won't be put out!" Vivica shouted.

"Vivica! Would you please just leave?" Pastor Miller was exasperated.

Vivica stared at Pastor Miller before she finally left.

"I have never seen her act like that before." Deacon

Edwards spoke.

"She acted a fool before she left the house earlier today." Mother Miller shared.

"This is so out of character for her. It's obvious that she's not herself." Marva Campbell added.

"She's burning bridges and she doesn't even realize it." Mother Miller said.

Robyn began pacing and clenching her fists. She punched her right fist into her left hand and paced a few more seconds before addressing Pastor Miller.

"I haven't been in church as long as everyone else in here, so prayer is not the first thing that comes to my mind when something like this pops off! I'm ready to handle this the way the only way I know how."

"Fighting is never the answer." Marva Campbell reasoned.

"I don't know anything about you, Sis. Marva, but I'm the youngest of eight girls and I've always had to fight." Robyn told her.

"There's not going to be any fighting. We need to pray." Pastor Miller interjected.

"Vivica had better put the cuckoo back in the clock before somebody shows her what time it is." Mother Miller added.

"Mom, don't let her bad attitude change you. You're better than that." Pastor Miller spoke calmly to his mother before addressing Deacon Edwards. "Deac, I'm going to make an appointment with your brother, so let him know to expect a call from me."

"Yes, sir, pastor. I'll call him tonight." Deacon Edwards assured him.

"I'll close us in prayer. I want to thank you for continuing to show your love and support." Pastor Miller expressed his gratitude to the Board members before he began praying.

"You're welcome." Everyone answered.

"Let us bow our heads. *Father, we thank you for letting Your word be a lamp unto our feet and a light unto our path. We're grateful that You continually show us Your grace and love, even in the smallest details of our lives. Please send us from this place with the assurance that You will never leave us without a Comforter. We will Honor Your Name forever and ever. Amen!"*

Everyone responded with a quiet, "Amen," before hugging him tightly as they each left the meeting room. Deacon Edwards stayed and turned off the lights throughout the church and ensured the windows and all doors were secure. As soon as Pastor Miller set the alarm, he and Deacon Edwards exited the church and shook hands before starting their cars and leaving the parking lot.

Pastor Miller drove home in silence. When he pulled into the driveway and pressed his garage opener to lift the garage door, he saw Vivica's car was parked in its regular spot. Almost immediately, he pressed the garage door opener again to close the garage door. He slowly backed out of the driveway. He wasn't ready to deal with her yet. He wasn't sure where he was going; he simply knew that he didn't want to be in her presence.

Pastor Miller drove for almost four hours before he finally exited the freeway and pulled into the parking lot of a popular hotel chain. He sat in the car for a few minutes, reflecting on the events of the past 24 hours. He felt defeated, but in his heart, he knew he wasn't.

He finally got out of his car and walked across the parking lot and entered the hotel lobby. The clerk at the front desk was very hospitable. Her huge smile reminded him of his daughter, Jaden. Thinking of Jaden made him sad. The revelation that Vivica had two other children really shook Jaden to her core. Pastor Miller thanked the hotel clerk when she handed him the keycard for the room that he rented for the night. He wasn't quite sure what the next day would bring, but he was ready to rest his body and his mind.

He took the elevator to the third floor and quickly found his room at the end of the hallway. When he opened the door, he was pleasantly surprised by how large the room was and he was thrilled that there was a Jacuzzi tub in the room. He wasted no time getting in it. He thought to himself how great life would be if trouble and sadness could go down the drain with the water. He enjoyed the serenity and looked forward to turning in for the night.

Meanwhile, Vivica and Mother Miller were in their respective bedrooms, purposely avoiding one another. Vivica began flipping through channels on the TV until she fell asleep. Mother Miller fell asleep working on a crossword puzzle.

Chapter Eleven

The next day Jaden was pacing back and forth in her apartment. She looked at the clock on the microwave and got extremely nervous when she realized Darrelle and Simone would be there any moment. She had invited them over to talk, so they could get acquainted and get to know one another. She wondered why she was so nervous. They were her siblings.

She had been in the kitchen for the past hour or so, preparing a special menu of pan seared sea bass with citrus salsa, scallops, rosemary roasted potatoes, and a wilted spinach salad. Simone had offered to bring something for dessert. As soon as she set the table, her doorbell rang. She took a deep breath before opening the door. Darrelle and Simone hugged her as she welcomed them in to her apartment.

She invited them to sit down. "Thank you both for meeting with me. I have so many questions that I don't even know where to start." Jaden told them.

"We have a lot of questions, too. What can you tell us

about your mom? I mean, our mom? What is she like? I want to know where I get some of my habits from. I crinkle my nose when I'm mad and I am very quiet until I get to know people." Simone replied.

"Simone, chill. You're doing too much." Darrelle admonished her.

"I can't help it. I want to know all I can about her." Simone told him.

"It's ok, Darrelle. Well, Mom has a heart of gold. She gives and gives and never asks for anything from anybody. She is strong and she takes good care of my dad. She has been a great example of unconditional love. She really loves without limitations," Jaden told them.

"You must mean she loves strangers. She never did anything for us." Darrelle responded angrily.

"That's enough, Darrelle." Simone touched his arm to calm him.

"Let me finish, Simone. Jaden needs to hear this, because it sounds like she's been loving and kind to everybody, except us!" He added.

"I'm sorry for what she did." Jaden told him.

"Don't apologize for her! She needs to apologize for herself!" Darrelle shouted.

"I understand your frustration, and although I'm upset with her, too, I get a little defensive about other people saying anything negative about her!" Jaden shouted back.

"Jaden, stop! We're not just other people! We're her kids, too!" Darrelle interrupted her.

"I get it. I'm sorry." She responded.

It's not your fault, Jaden. It's ok." Simone assured her.

"No, you don't get it!" Darrelle corrected her. "Until

you've walked in our shoes and have been through the crap we went through, you won't get it. OK?"

"Understood." Jaden conceded.

"Mothers are supposed to love their children unconditionally and protect them. She left us to fend for ourselves! To this day, I can still hear Simone crying and saying she was hungry. I was six years old and she was looking to me to feed her. What could I do? I was six! What could I do?" Darrelle raised his voice at Jaden.

"Darrelle, stop!" Simone pleaded.

"No, she needs to hear this!" He raised his voice. "While she was living the life of a precious little princess with Miss Vivica, we were sitting in the dark by ourselves, with no electricity and no food!" He stood up and continued raising his voice. "I was six years old and I was scared." He lowered his voice as a single tear rolled down his cheek.

"Darrelle, please stop." Simone put her arm around him in an attempt to comfort him.

He moved away from Simone and continued. '"Do you know what it's like on Mother's Day when all the kids are painting pictures to give to their mothers but you're wondering what you did wrong to make your mother leave?" He asked Jaden.

"I don't." She answered quietly.

"It's hell. That's what it is. No matter how many times a child is disappointed and hurt, they still love mama, no matter how deeply they've been hurt." He reasoned.

"Darrelle, I may not be able to relate to what you've gone through, but I want you to know I care." Jaden assured him. What do you want from my mother? I'm sorry. I mean from our mother." Jaden asked.

"I don't want anything!!" He told her. After a moment of silence, he told her, "I take that back. I only want one thing. I just want her to apologize! I don't even want to know why she left. I want her to apologize. That's it. Period. Point. Blank."

"Thank you for being so transparent, Darrelle." Jaden said.

"He can be brutally honest, but that's one of the many things I love about him." Simone laughed.

"I'm learning!" Jaden agreed.

"I didn't mean to be harsh, but I needed to get that off my chest." Darrelle explained.

"Its fine, Darrelle. You've enlightened me and I'm glad you did." Jaden hugged him and Simone.

"Whatever you cooked smells good. I hope you can't hear my stomach growling!" Darrelle teased. "Everything is ready. I hope you like sea bass and scallops."

"We both love seafood!" Simone smiled.

"Darrelle, I would be honored if you would bless the food." Jaden said.

"I'd be happy to do so. Let us bow:

"Father, Thank You for this wonderful food that you've provided for us. Let it be nourishing to our bodies. Bless us now as we fellowship with one another. Lord, I also want to say thank You for bringing us together today to share our hearts and thoughts with one another. Continue to bless us as we heal and get to know one another. In Your Name we pray, Amen."

Darrelle, Jaden and Simone continued to talk and share laughs over dinner. Jaden prepared a pot of coffee to go with Simone's homemade carrot cake.

Each of them knew this day was the beginning of an unbreakable bond between them.

Chapter Twelve

Early the next morning Pastor Miller showered and put on the same clothes from the day before. He planned to check out of the hotel and leave early enough to go home to change clothes. He and Vivica had a 10 a.m. counseling session with Dr. Edwards, Deacon Edwards' brother, and he didn't want to be late.

The long drive home was quiet. He didn't turn on the stereo. He needed time to think. He wasn't sure if the counseling session would help, but he was willing to go and listen to any advice Dr. Edwards offered.

He got off the freeway and turned left onto his street and into his driveway. He parked his car and went in the house. When he walked in, Vivica was already dressed. She was sitting at the dining nook, reading a magazine and sipping hot tea. He was expecting her to ask him where he had spent the night, but to his surprise, she was pleasant.

"Good morning, James," she greeted him.

"Good morning," he responded. As he turned to head upstairs to change his clothes, Vivica set her teacup down.

"Do you want to ride to the counseling appointment together?" she asked.

After a long silence, he finally answered, "That's fine with me."

He went upstairs and changed clothes and returned to find Vivica sitting quietly and staring off into space.

"A penny for your thoughts," he pried, in an attempt to break the silence.

"Nothing. I'm ready when you are."

Vivica walked out as Pastor Miller went to his mother's room to let her know they were leaving.

When they walked to the car, he instinctively opened the door for Vivica, just as he had done for the last 30 years.

Neither of them said anything while enroute to their counseling session. Fortunately, traffic was lighter than normal, so they arrived at Dr. Edwards' office fairly quickly. The office was easy to find. It was near LAX airport, in the city of Inglewood.

Pastor Miller parked in an unmarked stall in the office parking lot. He turned off the engine, took the key out of the ignition and got ready to walk around to Vivica's door to open it for her, but she had already opened the door and was stepping out of the car. He stepped aside to give her room to exit the passenger side and then closed the door behind her.

They walked into the medical building where Dr. Edwards' office was located and opened the door that led to his waiting room. The waiting room was simple, but beautifully decorated. To the left was a large mural depicting the breathtaking orange, red and yellow glow of a sun setting over a rippling lake. The lake reflected the colors cast upon it and reflected tints of orange, red and yellow.

To the right was a large, built-in aquarium. Dr. Edwards believed the aquarium would be a tranquil distraction for patients waiting to be seen.

When the Millers had signed in, the receptionist handed them a clipboard and paperwork to obtain their insurance information and health history. There were two other couples waiting to be seen by other counselors. Less than 5 minutes after they sat down, Darrelle and Simone arrived, and shortly afterwards, Jaden came in. Although the setting wasn't ideal, Pastor Miller was happy to see them, especially Jaden. She hadn't returned any of his calls since the incident a few nights prior. Everyone quietly greeted one another. Vivica was visibly nervous. She picked up a magazine and began thumbing through it quickly.

A few minutes passed before the receptionist announced that Dr. Edwards was ready to meet with Pastor and Mrs. Miller. The receptionist advised Darrelle, Jaden and Simone that Dr. Edwards wanted to speak to their parents alone and then he would call them in.

The walls in the hallway leading to Dr. Edwards' office were painted light blue. There were several framed commendations from local officials, acknowledging Dr. Edwards' community involvement, as well as his commitment to mental health awareness.

Dr. Edwards was standing behind his desk when the receptionist escorted them in. They shook hands and introduced themselves.

"Come on in and have a seat," he said. He noticed that Pastor Miller was staring at him.

"Is everything ok, Mr. Miller?" Dr. Edwards asked Pastor

Miller.

"Yes, everything is fine. I apologize for staring, but I forgot that you and Deacon Edwards were twins," Pastor Miller replied.

"Be sure to let my brother know you finally met the good looking twin," Dr. Edwards joked.

"I sure will," Pastor Miller smiled.

"The goal of this counseling session is to help each of you identify how your behavior affects others. Hopefully you'll learn new ways of relating to each other so that you can effectively resolve conflicts, and learn to communicate with one another." He offered. "What we discuss may get a little uncomfortable, but I'm asking that you keep an open mind and commit to not being judgmental. Agreed?" he asked.

The Millers shook their heads in agreement.

Dr. Edwards then turned his attention to Vivica.

"Mrs. Miller. I'll start with you. What's the reason you and your family are here today?" He asked.

Vivica shifted uncomfortably in her chair before speaking.

"It's a little complicated." She spoke, while trying to suppress a cough.

"It's ok. Take your time," Dr. Edwards assured her.

Vivica inhaled deeply before she spoke again.

"When I was 19 years old, I found myself in an abusive relationship. I got pregnant and ended up getting hooked on crack cocaine. I had two kids that I couldn't take care of and I felt overwhelmed." She began to cry, and stopped talking until she regained her composure.

"I walked out of my apartment one day to get high. I'm ashamed to admit this, but I didn't go back." She paused for a while before continuing. "Devin was 6 and Mya was 3 when I left. I got clean and I went back to look for them, but the state had already placed them in the foster care system." She cried softly.

Pastor Miller looked sympathetically at her, but didn't say anything.

"That was very brave of you to share so openly, Mrs. Miller." Dr. Edwards encouraged her.

"Thank you," she quietly responded.

"Would you mind sharing a little about your childhood?" Dr. Edwards asked.

"I was the middle of three children. I had an older brother and a younger sister. My dad died when I was eight years old. After he died, my mother did what she could to make ends meet. She always had to work two jobs to provide for us. My brother felt obligated to take care of us and my mother depended on him to protect us. My sister, Monique, was always sick and she was always in the hospital. I kept to myself and played with my dolls." Vivica looked down at her hands.

"Please continue, Mrs. Miller." Dr. Edwards said.

"My brother got a full scholarship to Grambling University, but the night before he left for college, he got robbed and killed three blocks from our house." Vivica inhaled deeply, before continuing. "My mother never recovered from my brother's death and the day he died, you could say that she stopped living, too." She paused to maintain her composure before continuing.

She committed suicide almost a year to the day after my brother died and I was the one who found her when I came home from school." She began to cry quietly.

"How old were you when that happened?" Dr. Edwards asked.

"I was 12 years old. She took her life on my 12th birthday!" She yelled. "I didn't know what to feel, but I couldn't make myself cry."

"It sounds to me like that's when you began detaching yourself from the trauma you were experiencing. The medical term for what you experienced is Dissociative Identity Disorder, which is triggered by a traumatic experience. You shut down so that you wouldn't feel anything," Dr. Edwards told her.

"When I lost my mother, everything changed." She stared at her hands.

"This is the first time I've heard any of this. When we met, you told me that your mom died of a heart attack." Pastor Miller interjected.

"How do you tell someone that your mother killed herself?" Vivica shouted.

"I am not just someone, Vivica. I'm your husband! You've lied about everything!" He shouted back and shook his head in disgust.

"I'm sorry," Vivica replied solemnly.

"Save it!" he fired back.

"Mr. Miller, you do know that it took a lot for her to be so transparent about her past, right?" Dr. Edwards asked.

"Yes, I realize that, but Vivica's been full of surprises and secrets these past few days, so if I sound insensitive, that's the reason. I'm afraid of what else may fall out of her closet. She's been misleading everybody for years." He replied.

"Why don't you share what you're feeling right now?" Dr. Edwards directed his question to Pastor Miller.

"Betrayed. Foolish. Hurt. Misled. Pick one." He answered sarcastically.

"Under these circumstances, each of those emotions is very normal. Let's shift the conversation and talk a little bit about your childhood, if you don't mind." Dr. Edwards said.

Pastor Miller shifted slightly in his seat before speaking.

"I think my childhood was pretty normal. My father was a preacher and my mom stayed home to raise me and my younger brother, Doug. My father died about 10 years ago and my mother came to live with us a year ago when she was undergoing chemo for breast cancer.

"Do you think your father being a minister had any influence over you going into ministry"? Dr. Edwards asked.

"To be honest, I don't think so. I did everything in my power to avoid the pulpit before I answered the call to ministry. When I couldn't deny the calling on my life, I stopped running and gave in." He paused before continuing. "In my early twenties, I ran as far away from the church as I could. You name it, I did it. I dabbled in drug dealing, hanging out with gang members, strong arm robbery, gun running. I left no stone unturned," he added.

Dr. Edwards scribbled a few notes in his notepad and thanked Pastor Miller for his honesty. Vivica continued staring at her hands.

Dr. Edwards called his receptionist and asked her to bring in Darrelle, Jaden and Simone.

They sat in silence while waiting for Darrelle, Jaden and Simone. Vivica didn't make eye contact with her children when they came in, although each of them looked at her when they entered the room. Vivica's eyes were red and swollen from crying.

"I'm glad that everyone made this counseling session a priority today. It's very important that you remember that there are a lot of layers to peel back and healing will take some time," Dr. Miller started. "Please understand that people can't change immediately, so I'm asking you to be patient with one another as you work toward reconciliation, which is the ultimate goal. Is everyone clear about the objective?" He asked.

Everyone shook their heads in agreement.

"Mrs. Miller, I'm going to allow you talk to your children and share with them what they don't know about you," Dr. Miller said.

Vivica sat quietly for a few seconds, wringing her hands together. "I shared with Dr. Edwards that I was a drug addict for years and, this is not an excuse, but my addiction caused me to make choices that I'm not proud of." She said. "The worst mistake I made was leaving you two." She looked remorsefully at Darrelle and Simone. "I thought about you every day." She continued. "On your birthdays, I whispered a prayer and asked God to watch over you, wherever you were." Tears began streaming down her face. Instinctively, Simone reached over and touched her mother's hand. Vivica looked at her and began to cry loudly. Jaden got up and hugged her mom. Darrelle looked at Pastor Miller, as though he was looking for answers.

"Darrelle, it's okay to comfort your mother." Dr. Edwards said.

"I'm good, Dr. Edwards." Darrelle responded.

"Why don't you tell me what you're feeling right now?" Dr. Edwards asked.

"Honestly? My emotions are all over the place. I'm

angry. I'm hurt. I'm confused." He replied.

"If your mother could give you one thing right now, what would you want from her?" Dr. Edwards asked.

"I don't need anything from her." He answered quickly.

Everyone sat silently.

Dr. Edwards looked at his watch and realized it was almost time for his next appointment.

"Unfortunately we're at the end of our session, but I do want to continue this dialog. I would like to have you come back the day after tomorrow, so please let my receptionist know what time you can come back on Wednesday or Thursday. In the meantime, I want everyone to be aware of how you speak to one another. If you find yourself getting angry or short with one another, please take a break and speak to another when you're less emotional." Dr. Edwards encouraged everyone as he made eye contact with each of them.

"Mr. and Mrs. Miller, your assignment is to take turns praying for one another at least once a day. You'll find that as you build one another up, it won't be so easy to tear one another down. Can you both commit to doing that for the next two days?" Dr. Edwards asked.

The Millers slowly nodded their heads in agreement.

"Darrelle, Jaden and Simone, I'm going to ask each of you to buy a journal or a notepad and jot down your emotions and how you're feeling at various times throughout the day. Nobody will read your notes, so be as honest as possible. Then, I'd like for each of you to go a step further and write a letter to Vivica. Take time to think through what you want to say to her. Are there any questions and is everyone clear on what your assignment is?" He asked.

Everyone agreed they were clear on the assignments Dr. Edwards had given them and they each stood up and shook hands with him as they got ready to leave his office.

"It was nice meeting everyone. Please allow me to pray for you before you leave." Dr. Edwards said.

"Lord, we would like to take this moment to thank You for the beauty and sanctity of marriage. We thank You for these three adult children who stand here today. Continue to bless them and keep and remind them of who they are in You. Guide their steps and keep them in Your loving care. Draw everyone close to one another during the difficult seasons of life. Restore peace in their home and let them reflect Your love, hope, and truth. I ask this In the Name that is above all Names. Amen."

Pastor Miller shook the doctor's hand. "Thank you for your time, Dr. Edwards. We'll see you in a couple of days."

The family stopped at the receptionist's desk and scheduled a follow-up appointment.

They exited the building and said their goodbyes as they walked toward the parking lot to get in their cars. Darrelle, Jaden and Simone hugged Pastor Miller. They looked at Vivica and each of them seemed reluctant to hug her, but they did so anyway. Surprisingly, Darrelle hugged Vivica tightly, as if he didn't want to let her go. Vivica hugged him tighter.

Pastor Miller opened Vivica's door and she thanked him as she got in the car. He closed her door and walked around to the driver's side, and got in. He started the engine and drove toward home. They drove home in silence. Pastor

Miller felt they had a good counseling session, but he wasn't quite ready to fully let his guard down.

When they arrived home, he went to his home office to start preparing the weekly Bible study lesson. Vivica went upstairs to change clothes. She returned a short time later and set the table before heating some leftovers. She called out to James to let him know dinner was ready. He joined her at the table. There was an awkward silence between them, but Vivica was hopeful that this was a step in the right direction.

They both prayed silently before they ate.

When they finished eating, James cleared the table and loaded the dishwasher.

Vivica thanked him for loading the dishwasher and then she caught him off guard by asking him if he wanted to watch a movie with her. He hesitated, but gave in.

He chuckled when he realized Vivica had chosen, "Jumping the Broom" for them to watch. This was one of her favorite movies and she watched it at least once a month.

When the movie ended, he made sure the doors were locked and the alarm was set. They went upstairs and got ready for bed. Before they turned off the lights, Pastor Miller asked Vivica if he could pray for her. His request touched her deeply. They knelt beside the bed, bowed their heads and held hands.

"Thank you, Father, for being a shield around us. We know the enemy comes to steal, kill and destroy, but we thank You for giving us Your love in abundance.

When the enemy of her soul tells her she's defeated, bring your Word to her mind as you strengthen her and help her fight the good fight of faith. Remind her of the victory that we have through

You.

We know that nothing can separate us from Your unconditional love. We pray that you continue to keep us in Your loving care. Amen."

"Amen," Vivica spoke quietly. "That was beautiful. I'd love to pray for you now."

"I'd love that," Pastor Miller smiled.

"God, you've created James in Your image, and I know that You've set him apart for greatness," she started.

"Thank You for making him a mighty man of valor, who is strong in his faith and committed to Your will.

You've made him a great protector for our family and I feel safe with him. Give him the courage and wisdom that he needs to make decisions that honor You. Please fulfill all the plans You have for him.

Please show me how to be supportive and encouraging. Bind us together as one and strengthen the bond between us each day. Amen"

They hugged one another while they were still on their knees. Their unconditional love for one another was rekindled that night.

The next couple of days they were intentional about showing kindness to one another and genuinely listening to one another as they went about their daily routine.

On the day of their follow up appointment with Dr. Edwards, Pastor Miller got up early and cooked breakfast. Vivica could smell bacon cooking when she woke up, so she showered, got dressed and went downstairs. She was pleasantly surprised to find that James had prepared a hearty breakfast of scrambled eggs, turkey bacon, smothered potatoes and toast.

"It's been a long time since you've cooked. You've still got the magic touch, sir" she teased. "Is your mom joining us?" she asked.

"Mom left about an hour. She said she was going on a bus trip with the senior group at the community center. She'll be gone until later this evening."

"I remember now. She mentioned that to me a couple of days ago, but I forgot. I didn't even hear you get out of bed. I guess I was more tired than I thought."

"You were sleeping peacefully so I thought I'd surprise you and cook for you to give you a break from the kitchen."

"Good job. Thank you," she said.

When they finished eating, they headed to their appointment with Dr. Edwards.

The waiting room was pretty full. The kids were already signed in and seated. Everyone seemed happy and relaxed as they laughed and talked with one another. The receptionist called them back shortly after they arrived.

They were engaged in small talk when Dr. Edwards came in.

"I apologize for being late. My previous appointment ran a little long," he started. I'm going to dig into some places that may get a little uncomfortable, but trust the process and I promise it'll be worth it. Let's get started."

"Why don't we start with you, Jaden?" He suggested.

"These past couple of weeks have been interesting, but in a good way. Finding out that I had a brother and a sister was a shock, to say the least. We spent some time together over the weekend, getting to know one another. I'm glad to have them in my life, but I'm still trying to get my head around all this."

"That's understandable. It's a lot to take in." Dr. Edwards assured her.

"I just want things to be the way they were. My mom's secret affected everyone's life." She continued.

"Thank you for your honesty. Simone, why don't you go next?"

Simone inhaled deeply.

"Well, luckily for me, I don't remember when my mom left. I remember Darrelle and I being in foster care for a while until I got adopted. I remember the day that I had to leave foster care without Darrelle. I cried all night. My adoptive parents were good to me, but I missed Darrelle. They always treated me very well. They always encouraged me to look for my birth parents, but I never was ready to open that chapter of my life, but I'm glad that we found Mom. I feel like my life is complete now." She smiled and put Vivica's hand in hers.

"Thank you, Simone. Darrelle, let's hear from you."

"I've never really opened up and talked about this, so give me moment." Darrelle stated. "The first couple of foster families that took me in were pretty good to me. The last foster family I was in was the worst. My foster mother told me that the only reason she let me stay was because she needed the money. She said she didn't even like kids. Do you have any idea what that does to a child?" He looked at Vivica and continued. "If a mother doesn't love her own kids, why would anyone else be expected to do so?" Darrelle's bottom lip began to quiver, as he tried to hold back his tears.

"Take your time, Darrelle. You can finish whenever you're ready." Dr. Edwards said.

"All I ever wanted was to be loved. All these years I have grieved for what I never had. I was so confused when I was growing up. I didn't know how to love. I found myself using this woman and that woman and going from relationship to relationship. I never stayed in a relationship long enough to care about the person I was with and I never allowed myself to have feelings for anybody. The truth is I was always secretly looking for love that I never found." Darrelle said.

Vivica looked at Darrelle and then finally got up and sat down next to him and put her arm around his shoulder. He stood up and walked away from her and walked over to the window.

Everyone sat quietly.

"I've hated you my entire life. I want to hate you now. I feel like I need to hate you now, but when I look in your eyes, it makes me mad and confused about how I feel." He said, while looking out of the window.

"You don't have to hate her. It's ok to allow yourself to love her." Dr. Edwards said.

"I don't think I'm ready yet." Darrelle said.

Vivica, Simone and Jaden were crying silently. Pastor Miller got up and put his arms around all three of them while Darrelle continued standing by the window.

"I'm going to give you all some privacy and a chance to connect." Dr. Edwards got up to leave.

"Thank you for your help, Dr. Edwards." Pastor Miller shook his hand.

"You're welcome. I'll be in my office, so let me know if you need anything.

Everyone was talking quietly among themselves and

consoling one another, when Vivica had a coughing spell. Dr. Edwards gave her a bottle of water before he closed the door and went to his office.

"I'm so sorry for the pain that I've caused everyone. I pray and hope that each one of you will find it in your hearts to forgive me. I know it will take some time, but please think about it. If you give me a chance, I can prove to you that I'm not the same woman who walked out and left you. I hope that one day you can at least think about forgiving me."

"I don't know if I can forgive you. Our lives were turned upside down when you left." Darrelle told her.

"I can't undo the past, but I promise if you give me a chance, I'll do what I can to make it up to you. I know that saying I'm sorry doesn't seem like much, but it's a start."

"Darrelle, I know you've been hurt and I know this is a lot to take in, but I'll be here for you. I'm willing to work through this with you. The Bible tells us to do all we can to live peacefully with others and to forgive as God forgives us." Pastor Miller told him.

Darrelle was quiet for several seconds.

"I'll try." He said.

Everyone was relieved that Darrelle was willing to forgive Vivica. No one was foolish enough to think everything would be 100% perfect or that they would always see eye-to-eye on everything, but they were willing to work it out.

They each left Dr. Edwards' office with renewed faith, believing everything would be fine in due time.

When they got home, Vivica said she was tired and needed a nap. She promised to make lunch when she got up.

James told her that was fine with him, because he needed

to work on his sermon. He retreated to his home office. Before he realized it, two and a half hours had passed and Vivica poked her head in his office.

"I made lunch for us. Are you able to break away and join me?"

"I'll take a break and join you. I'll go wash up." Vivica walked back to the kitchen.

Pastor Miller walked in just as she was setting his plate down.

"This looks good." He said.

"It's that Jamaican Jerk Chicken that you like."

"My, my, my. I can't wait to dig in. Let's pray." He reached across the table to hold her hand. He remembered what Dr. Edwards said about praying out loud for one another as he began praying.

"Father, we ask for Your blessings now as we prepare to eat. Thank You for always providing for us. Let this food nourish our bodies and let our kindness toward one another nourish our souls. I would also like to take this time to lift my wife up to You, Lord. Heal Vivica's brokenness and fill her with the love, comfort and peace that only You can give. On days when she feels unloved, let her know how much she's loved and needed. I pray this in Your Name. Amen".

"Hearing you say my name while you're praying really humbles me," she told him while suppressing a cough. "Let me pray for you."

"Dear Lord, Your Word says it is not good for a man to be alone and that he who finds a wife finds a good thing. I thank You for allowing James to find me and for making us partners in life. Bless James and keep him in Your care. Continue to guide his steps. I pray these blessings over his life. Amen."

They stared into one another's eyes and after a few seconds of silence, they ate.

"This is really good." He said between bites. "It's been a long time since you made this."

"Thank you. Since you like it so much, I'll make it more often. Deal?"

"Deal."

"Do you want to get some coffee and dessert when we finish eating?" He asked her.

"That would be nice. It's been a while since we've been out for coffee."

They talked and even laughed during the short ride to one of their favorite restaurants. Pastor Miller held open the heavy glass door and allowed Vivica to enter ahead of him. Understandably, there had been a lot of tension between them since Darrelle had confronted her; Vivica was nervous, but hopeful that the counseling sessions and prayer and communication would help them move toward reconciliation. As always, the restaurant was crowded, but they were seated quickly. They reviewed the menu and ordered slices of their favorite pies and coffee.

While waiting for their order, they continued to talk and both consented to recommit to their marriage and continue counseling sessions with Dr. Edwards. They agreed that their marriage was worth fighting for and they were both willing to do so.

When they left the restaurant, Pastor Miller suggested they walk along the beach to watch the sunset. Vivica smiled as this was something she loved to do, but due to their busy schedules, it had been at least a year since they had done so. There was a slight breeze, so Pastor Miller put his arm around his wife to keep her warm. She nestled in close and inhaled deeply and slowly exhaled. Neither of them wanted the moment to end.

When they got home, they spent the evening cuddled up on the couch, talking and listening to jazz. They fell asleep on the couch. Pastor Miller woke up Vivica around 2:00 AM and encouraged her to come up to bed.

Chapter Thirteen

Five months later, New Year's Eve

Pastor Miller and his mother were busy setting the table for dinner in the family room, while Jaden was in the kitchen putting appetizers on serving platters. Vivica had done most of the cooking, but she felt a little dizzy earlier, so Pastor Miller encouraged her to lie down for a few minutes. They were expecting Darrelle and Simone to join them to ring in the New Year. They were both bringing dates with them.

"The Good Lord knows that I am happy to see this year come to an end. We've had our share of challenges these past few months, but a new year means a new beginning." Mother Miller said.

"I agree, mom. These past few months have been extremely difficult, but I thank God that He has walked with us through every storm and carried us when we got weak. I believe the New Year will bring unexpected blessings." Pastor Miller said.

"All I know is that God is a promise-keeper. I asked Him

to move like never before and He did just that. He never fails!" She smiled.

"Daddy, I'm glad you and mom decided to put everything behind you and stay together." Jaden said, while setting a covered basket of warm dinner rolls on the table.

"I am, too, baby." Pastor Miller put his arm around Jaden's shoulder and kissed her on the forehead.

They were interrupted when the doorbell rang.

Mother Miller hugged everyone and welcomed them to come in. Simone brought a date, a quiet and handsome young man named Jamaal, and happily introduced him.

"Where's Darrelle?" Mother Miller asked Simone.

"He's running late, but he just sent a text saying he would be here shortly."

Everyone was talking, laughing and snacking on an array of appetizers.

Darrelle rang the doorbell and as everyone had expected, he brought Keenya with him.

They had been dating exclusively for almost two years and everyone loved her quiet presence and they believed she was perfect for him.

A few minutes after Darrelle and Keenya arrived, Vivica came downstairs and joined everyone. She was overcome with emotion and started crying.

Pastor Miller walked over to her and hugged her.

"This is a day for rejoicing. Not tears." He comforted her, while wiping the tears from her face.

"These are tears of joy." She assured him, while suppressing a cough.

"It's been said that whatever you're doing when the New Year comes in, that's what you'll do all year." He pulled her in closer.

"I hope that's true." She coughed a few more times.

"I know you saw Dr. Douglas a couple of days ago. Did she say if you have bronchitis again?" He asked her.

Vivica took a deep breath, before answering. "No."

"Did she say what's causing that cough?"

"Yes." She wiped a tear.

"What did she say?"

"We'll talk later. Let's enjoy the New Year celebration."

"This is the perfect way to end the year. Family is everything." Mother Miller handed each of them a champagne flute filled with sparkling cider. "Mom, when I was growing up, you taught me that a family that prays together stays together."

"Prayer is the most powerful resource a Christian family has, yet, so many families have gotten away from certain traditions. Instagram and Snapchat have replaced family Bible Study and family devotions."

"Granny, what do you know about Instagram and Snapchat?" Jaden asked.

"Jaden, I haven't been old all my life. She looked over her glasses before continuing. "Hash tag: I'm just sayin'".

Everyone laughed.

"Granny! Please don't say 'hashtag' anymore." Jaden laughed.

"Hash tags were tic, tac, toe tables back in the day." Mother Miler responded.

"We called them number signs in my day." Vivica added.

"There's nothing new under the sun. You young people think you invented everything. I thought the same thing when I was growing up." Mother Miller said.

"Listen, everybody. They're getting ready to drop the ball." Simone interrupted.

Everyone gathered around the television to watch the ball drop at Madison Square and they counted down in unison: 10, 9, 8, 7, 6, 5, 4, 3, 2, 1. Happy New Year!

Jaden and Simone blew their party horns, while James kissed Vivica.

"Darrelle walked over to Vivica and said, "Happy New Year, mom."

"I've waited almost 30 years to hear those words from you. Happy New Year, baby." She hugged Darrelle and kissed him on the cheek.

Everyone hugged one another and clicked their glasses together.

"Thanks for inviting me to celebrate the New Year with you and your family," Jamaal told Simone as they hugged.

"These past few months have been crazy. I really can't believe we found her. I thank God for putting all the puzzle pieces together for my family." Simone replied.

"I know you probably think that I wouldn't be able to relate to you, since I grew up with both of my parents, but, if you ever need someone to talk to, I'm here for you." Jamaal assured her.

"I appreciate that." Simone leaned her head on his chest.

Their quiet moment was interrupted when Darrelle spoke. "Can I get everyone's attention, please?"

Everyone quieted down.

"I want to say how blessed I am to start this New Year off with all the people I love." He said.

"We love you, too." Everyone said in unison.

"I'm praying for this New Year to be filled with love and

new beginnings. I want to share this New Year and the rest of my life with the woman I love." He said as he reached into his pocket and pulled out a ring box.

Keenya cupped both hands over her mouth.

Darrelle kneeled on one knee and reached out for Keenya's left hand.

"Keenya Yvonne Shephard, my life would be complete if you gave me the honor of being my wife. Will you marry me?"

Yes! Yes!" Keenya squealed.

Everyone clapped as Darrelle stood up and kissed Keenya. He put his hands around her waist and picked her up and spun her around.

Vivica, Mother Miller, Jaden and Simone gathered around Keenya to see and admire her ring and hug her.

Vivica waited for everyone else to hug her, before she hugged her.

"Welcome to the family, Keenya!"

"Thank you so much!"

"I'd like to toast to new beginnings." Simone said.

Everyone lifted their glasses and toasted the newly engaged couple.

Pastor Miller and Vivica stepped away from the crowd while everyone chatted.

Vivica kissed her husband on the cheek.

"I love you, James Miller."

"I love you more and don't ever forget that, Vivica."

As they embraced, they could hear, "Our Love" by Natalie Cole playing softly.

"James! That's the first song we danced to at our wedding reception!" Vivica exclaimed.

"I remember. I think that's a sign that we'll always be together." Pastor Miller said.

Vivica laid her head on his chest and they began slow dancing.

"Get a room!" Jaden joked.

"Come on. Let's give these lovebirds some privacy." Mother Miller ushered Jaden, Simone and Jamaal from the dining area to the family room. Darrelle and Keenya stayed and slowed danced together to the music.

While they danced, Darrelle whispered in Keenya's ear. "I promise to love you and treat you like the queen you are until death do us part."

"I'm going to hold you to that promise I pray that we have a love as strong as what your parents have." She told him.

"We will. They've been through hell and high water, but they've stood together and trusted God through it all." Darrelle said.

"One thing I know for sure is that we'll definitely come to them whenever we need prayer," Keenya told him.

Darrelle kissed Keenya gently.

"Absolutely." He told her.

Darrelle inhaled and exhaled deeply and squeezed Keenya's hand tightly.

"In a nutshell, that's my life. I hope this answers your question about my past. This is who I am," he told Keenya.

"I know it took a lot for you to be so vulnerable with me, Darrelle. I appreciate you trusting me enough to share so openly," she assured him.

"Now that all my skeletons are out of the closet, I hope that you're still willing to meet me at the altar and declare in front of God and our family and friends that you want to marry me and spend your life with me," Darrelle joked. "I hope my life story didn't scare you."

She held her left hand out at arms' length and admired her engagement ring before she responded.

"You have put a ring on it and I'm not going anywhere. I love you, Darrelle Brown. We're in this together. I'm with you until the wheels fall off." She immediately leaned over and laid her head on Darrelle's shoulder.

"I love you, too, babe," he told her. "Thank you for having my back. I'm glad I have someone in my corner that I trust unconditionally. We make a great team."

"Amen to that," she replied.

The rest of the night was filled with laughs, dinner and music.

The End

MisLeading Lady

Sharon Y. Judie

ABOUT THIS GUIDE

The questions are intended to enhance your group's enjoyment and reading of this book

1. Have you ever known someone with an addiction? If so, did their choices or lifestyle affect you? Were you able to separate them as a person from their actions? Why or why not?

2. When you read about Vivica's childhood during the counseling session, what emotions did you feel? Were you more understanding of why she abandoned her children? Why or why not?

3. Do you think your own childhood has had a positive or negative affect on you as an adult?

4. When Darrelle confronted Vivica, was he justified in doing so? What are your thoughts about how he confronted her? Have you ever had to confront someone from your past who did you wrong? Did you feel better once you confronted them?

5. When confronted about abandoning her children, Vivica initially felt bad, but she eventually started lashing out. Have you ever lashed out when you felt misunderstood? Did you apologize for how you acted? Was your apology sincere?

6. Mother-Daughter relationships can be tricky. Simone wanted to have a genuine relationship with her mother, Vivica, although Vivica had abandoned. How

has your relationship with your mother shaped any of your other relationships?

7. Vivica's other daughter, Jaden, respected and loved her mother (even when she was mad at her). Have you ever had to defend someone you loved? Do you feel there are any relationships that are not worth salvaging? Have you ever stayed in a relationship knowing it was over?

8. Darrelle mentioned a couple of times that he only wanted his mother to apologize. Is there someone you need to apologize to for your actions? Are you waiting for an apology from someone?

9. If someone who wronged you is no longer alive (or you no longer communicate with them) and you're harboring anger or unforgiveness, write a letter to them. Then burn it. Doing so may help you move on.

10. Family dynamics can be challenging. Do you have a family member that you need to forgive? Is there a family member who you wish would forgive you? How important is reconciliation to you?

11. Which character did you relate to most, and what was it about that character that made you connect with them?

12. Many people have secrets that they've never shared with anyone. Do you have a secret that you've been keeping? Do you think you'll ever share it?

13. Do you think it's acceptable if someone keeps a secret to protect their reputation? Why or why not?

14. Do you think it's acceptable to keep a secret to protect someone's feelings?

15. If this book were adapted into a movie, who would you want to see cast in the leading roles? Who would you cast as Pastor Miller and why? Who would you cast as Lady Vivica and why?

I'd love to hear your thoughts: Sharon.Judie@gmailcom

ABOUT THE AUTHOR

Sharon Y. Judie is a writer and inspirational speaker who has penned several stage plays, one murder mystery and more than a dozen skits, including the popular monologue series, "Women of the Bible Speak to Today's Women". Always seeking to encourage and mentor youth, Sharon hosts the "Dare to Dream Empowerment Summit", an annual conference for teens being raised without their father in the home. She published her first book, "Heart to Heart: Encouragement, Advice and inspiration for Teen Girls", a compilation book of letters and advice, written to encourage teen girls. Sharon is the Founder of Ten Talents Productions an organization designed to Empower at risk youth through writing, creative and performing arts as well as mentorship programs.

Email: Sharon.Judie@gmail.com
Facebook.com/SharonYJudie
Twitter.com/SharonJudie1
Instragram.com/SharonYJudie